GABE'S FALL

AND OTHER CLIMBING STORIES

GABE'S FALL

AND OTHER CLIMBING STORIES

Peter Lars Sandberg

Diadem Books

British Library Cataloguing in Publication Data is available

ISBN 0 906371 63 5 (cased edition)
ISBN 0 906371 53 8 (trade pbk edition)

Copyright © 1990 by Peter Lars Sandberg

Published in Great Britain in 1990 (in cased and
tradepaper editions) by Diadem Books Ltd, London

First published in 1988 by Birchfield Books
North Conway, New Hampshire, USA

Trade enquiries to Hodder and Stoughton
Mill Road, Dunton Green, Sevenoaks, Kent TN13 2YA

Printed and bound in Great Britain by
Biddles Ltd, Guildford and King's Lynn

This book is for Nancy

*Who has shared the rope
for over thirty years*

With love

CONTENTS

INTRODUCTION

When I first met Peter Sandberg in the fall of 1958, neither of us was a climber. We both were graduate students at the University of Colorado in Boulder, aiming for master's degrees in English and American literature. I wanted to be a teacher; Peter wanted to be a writer and a teacher of writing. Another student, Prince Wilmon, taught me to climb and I shared my new knowledge with Peter.

Peter and his wife Nancy lived in a small stone cottage near the mouth of Boulder Canyon, an easy walk from good granite cliffs. When I would go there to pick Peter up for a climb, I would sometimes find him writing, sometimes lifting weights.

I was prejudiced in favor of the first activity and against the second. This was a time when most climbers felt that climbing was the only necessary preparation for climbing. If a route required greater strength than I had, I grabbed slings. Peter made me more willing to train for rock climbing, and I sometimes joined him for a workout with the weights.

His writing was his real occupation, even when he was a student. His first published short story, which appeared in the U. of C. student literary magazine in 1958, was titled "Mountain to Climb." Since then he has published a number of novels, one with a mountaineering setting *(Wolf Mountain,* 1975) and many short stories. He also has been a book reviewer for *Saturday Review,* a magazine editor, and a teacher of writing at Northeastern University and at Holy Cross College. Recently he wrote a biography of President Dwight Eisenhower for young adult readers, which was published in 1986.

His story "Calloway's Climb" received the prestigious Foley Award for *Best American Short Stories* in 1974, and was made into a TV movie starring Mariette Hartley, Patrick O'Neal, and Mike Hoover as Calloway. Others of his stories have been anthologized, and several have been republished in other languages. Peter's writing career has attracted the interest of Boston University, which will include his papers in their Twentieth Century Archives collection.

In Peter's climbing stories the mountains and cliffs provide a setting for adventure and also for insights into real people. His stories are psychological, as well as physical, adventures. As I read his stories it is the action which keeps me turning the pages with constant pleasure, and the human situations which I continue to think about later. Those of us who climb mountains notice that people show their true natures more readily when climbing than during less stressful times. Decisions have to be made, and if a person is egotistical, or selfish, or unrealistic, his decisions may be wrong and dangerous. Such a decision changes the lives of the two characters in the title story of this collection, "Gabe's Fall."

One of the first things I noticed and liked about Peter was his deep interest in people's real selves. He has always wanted to understand the people he meets. Because of this his fictional characters have a human reality. When Hawsmoot decides to keep on climbing without a rope, we understand not only his decision but how he came to make that decision. When Elizabeth in "Calloway's Climb" decides to be unfaithful to her husband, we feel sympathy for her and for her husband. Peter is a moralist – not in the sense that he points his finger at immorality – but in that he allows us to better understand human nature and human values, even in a fast-paced adventure story like "B-Tower West Wall" or a comic story like "The Old Bull Moose of the Woods."

One aspect of the human condition which recurs in Peter's climbing stories is the process of aging. Time overtakes all of us, but for a mountaineer that overtaking is especially significant. In "The Devil's Thumb" a young climber comes to understand emotionally what it means to grow older. In "Hawsmoot" an eighteen year old climber feels invincible while a fifty-four year old solo climber faces the fact that he may die at his sport. In "The Rhyme of Lancelot" we get to look into the lives of an older man and woman, lives in which the climbing of an easy mountain is a way to remove themselves from the world and gain a larger perspective.

When Peter and I took up the sport of climbing, we liked it but did not consider giving it a primary place in our lives. Today there are many full-time climbers; then, I felt guilty when I put off working on my master's thesis to spend more time climbing. I never would have guessed that I would become a professional climber. I was sure however that Peter would be a professional writer and that he would continue to climb.

I was only partly right. Peter's active involvement with climbing came to an end four days before Christmas, 1962. He fell approximately sixty feet while leading a climb on the soft sandstone near Phoenix. After the fall Peter was unconscious and a bone was sticking out of his thigh. Bill Forrest was climbing in the area, and he and others lowered Peter to the ground from where he was carried to the highway and taken by ambulance to the hospital in Phoenix.

When he became conscious, Peter told Nancy that he probably wouldn't make it home from the hospital in time for Christmas. She burst into tears and told him that Christmas had already passed. Peter had been on the critical list, close to death and in a coma, for five days. His injuries kept him in the hospital for seven weeks, and it was over a year before he recovered.

Usually the climbing community doesn't hear from people who are forced to stop climbing because of a serious accident. We read about them in "Accidents in North American Mountaineering" and hope it never happens to us. But Peter was different – he was a writer who loved climbing and he had five good years to draw on. He had climbed in the mountains of Colorado, Wyoming, and Arizona, at Devil's Lake in Wisconsin and the Shawangunks in New York. He had also climbed isolated pinnacles like Shiprock and Devil's Tower. This collection of stories shows the importance of those experiences.

Peter continues to write, and currently is renovating a 90-year-old farmhouse in the Shenandoah Valley of Virginia, where Nancy is Division Chairman of Humanities at Blue Ridge Community College. They spend as much time as they can at their cottage on a lake in New Hampshire, where Peter has written many of the stories collected here.

I hope you enjoy them as much as I have. Good reading and good climbing.

George Hurley
Conway, New Hampshire
July, 1987

In December, 1962, I took a nearly fatal leader fall from a cliff in Arizona. I was stopped by my partner, Al Dutton, on a belaying ledge sixty feet above the ground. My wife, Nancy, after pulling me into a safer position, had to climb down from the ledge, without a rope, in order to go for help. I have always thought of this as very courageous on her part; and the situation she found herself in became, in a very general way, the seed for my story "Gabe's Fall."

Because of the seriousness of my accident and the concern of Nancy and my family, I gave up climbing for a long time. Then, in the autumn of 1979, I found I was having trouble trying to write a short story with a rock climbing setting. Techniques and equipment had changed; I needed a personal and present-day experience to help bring a rock climbing scene to life.

I called my old friend George Hurley and told him my problem. He happily suggested we do a climb together. The climb he chose was "Refuse" on Cathedral Ledge, a 500-foot cliff in North Conway, New Hampshire.

Going to the cliff that early morning in November, 1979, I was nervous. To me, Cathedral Ledge was intimidating, especially in light of what had happened to me my last time out.

Once I was on the climb, however, it felt familiar and right. George was steady and reassuring as my guide. The day was crisp and clear. By the time we stopped for lunch on a ledge high on the face, I was feeling all of the exhilaration I had always felt when climbing.

I promised Nancy my Cathedral Ledge climb would be my last. Of all the climbs I have done, it is the one I value most.

Written: Bow Lake, Strafford, New Hampshire; Summer, 1977

Revised: Bow Lake; Summer, 1987

"Gabe's Fall" has been purchased by *McCall's* magazine and is scheduled to appear in a future issue in a slightly different form.

GABE'S FALL

Secured to a ledge high on the face of a mountain cliff, Ruth Turner sat attending the rope that joined her to her fiancé Gabe. The ledge was narrow, and she sat facing out, could see the tops of the trees far below her and the straight long distance to the ground.

The rope was red. It ran from her small gloved hands on a sharp diagonal forty feet to the single chock and sling Gabe had fixed to the wall to protect himself, and from there ten feet higher to his waist. He was standing poised now on such small holds that when she craned her head up to watch him, she could see almost all of the cleated soles of his boots.

"Give me some slack!" he called, his voice sounding impatient. She released more of the rope in his direction, letting it slide across her back, then holding it firmly again. For the last ten minutes he had been trying to wedge his fingers into a thin crack that split the rock vertically just above his head. Until this point, he had climbed easily up from the ledge and was not far from the top of the cliff itself.

"Hey!" she called. "If it's getting that hard, let's forget it! We can rope down! We've done plenty for one day!"

"No!" he called back. "We're going to finish this!"

Annoyed, she shook her head. "We don't have to, you know!"

He did not reply, and though he did not fall just then, only jerked impatiently at the rope, it was in that moment she began to sense with a dread and increasing certainty that he was going to.

She was twenty-six, he was twenty-eight. They had met the previous summer in Boston at the publishing house where they worked, she as a copy editor, he in public relations. He had asked her to lunch one day and by the time they were eating dessert had told her he intended to marry her. She had been amused, but flattered too – offers from men as attractive and able as Gabe had not been pouring in. Most of the men who wanted to take her out were tedious on the subject of sex, and inept, and seemed to have little else on their minds.

Gabe was a doer. He planned trips and activities, introduced her to this sport and that, told her she was good at most of them – well co-ordinated – and this was something no one had told her before. She had been the middle child of a midwestern family with solid values and not much money, had had to pay her way through school with a number of small scholarships she had earned by studying hard. There had never been time for sailing or skiing or climbing cliffs, and one of the reasons she had grown to love Gabe was that he knew about these things and had seen to it she knew about them too. In this way, he had given her a new sense of herself, an added dimension. She had gotten used to thinking of Ruth Turner as a mildly bookish sort who on a good day could edit copy with the best of them. Then Gabe had come along and said, "Yes, yes, you *are* that; but you can be this too!"

He was a tall, pleasant looking man in a rugged sort of way, with reddish brown hair and blue eyes and a beard that seemed to pop into sight an hour or so after he shaved. He was outgoing and friendly, but very intense and aggressive too, and the more obviously liberated of the women at work had warned Ruth from the start he was irremediably macho and she better beware. She had listened to them in her quiet way, had decided finally she liked Gabe's masculine qualities and saw no reason to apologize for them. When it came to climbing cliffs – and, for that matter, doing lots of the things they enjoyed doing together – he simply preferred to lead, and she did not mind following.

The ledge was 300 feet above the ground, and the climb

to it had been strenuous and slow. They had moved in pitches of fifty and sixty feet, Gabe going first, protecting himself with his chocks and slings, then protecting her with the rope from above as she climbed each pitch to join him. She had carried their lunch in a small pack, and they had eaten on the ledge, which was only sixty feet from the top of the cliff itself. They had had jelly sandwiches and hard-boiled eggs and fresh green grapes which had stayed cool in the pack. She had sat away from the edge, with her back resting against the wall of the cliff. Gabe had sat with his legs dangling over, tossing grapes into the air and catching them in his mouth. When he missed one, he snatched for it and she caught her breath.

"Hate to waste a grape," he said, smiling.

"We've got lots of grapes," she said. "We've only got one of you."

He scooted back to sit beside her and at once she was aroused by his close presence, felt a prickling through her cheek which she hoped didn't show. It annoyed her sometimes that he could knock her off kilter this easily. He squinted up, as if to take the measure of what was left of the cliff.

"How about we make love before we finish this thing?" he said.

"You're not serious," she said.

"Sure am," he said. "It could be outstanding. We'd have the added element of risk, danger of rolling over the edge at a critical moment, hot sun beating down. I've been thinking about it ever since we got here."

"Well I've been thinking about the cottage we rented," she said. "Where we can go for a swim first, and have a drink."

"Much too conventional," he said.

"I am conventional. I've tried to tell you. It comes from having been raised in Indiana. Like an ear of corn."

He laughed, put his arms around her. She had worn short pants and a sleeveless jersey, and he put his hands under the jersey where her skin was slippery and warm.

"You're making me blush," she said.

"Nobody blushes these days," he said.

"I do," she said.

"That's why I love you," he said. "Because you're conventional, and you blush, and you're beautiful too."

"Only pleasant looking, my mother tells me."

"Your mother's a noodle," he said. "Tell me about the men in your life."

"I've told you," she said. "You're the man in my life."

"There must have been others. Before me."

"Just one or two along the way. They didn't amount to much."

He smiled as if he was glad to hear this, then he kissed her. She returned his kiss more eagerly than she had meant to. *"They didn't amount to much,"* she whispered, glancing toward the edge. *"God I'll be glad when we're off of here."*

It was mid-summer hot, and silent now around the ledge except for a hint of breeze and the dull scrabble of Gabe's boot on the wall above as he tried once again to move up from the tricky place he had reached. She craned her head to watch him, could see the clenched muscles of his legs and forearms as he tried to get his hands into the crack that began just above his head.

He had told her what to do in the unlikely event he should fall, and she tried to remember what he had said and what she had learned on the practice climbs they had done. They had rented a cottage for a week on the shore of a lake – a lovely small cottage with a grand fireplace, and no other cottages in sight – and Gabe had been at his best, creating atmospheres of candlelight and wine, introducing her to the pleasure of swimming without a suit, taking her in bed at night in his intense male way which if it left her more excited than satisfied also made her happy she had found someone to love at last who seemed to love her too.

"Gabe! Please!" she called.

"That's too much slack!" he called. "Take some back!"

She did, glancing up, feeling bits of grit he had dislodged sting her cheek and arm. He had talked her into wearing her shorts and she wished now she hadn't. They had hiked four miles from the lake to the cliff and the mosquitoes had been bad and now the rock was sharp under her legs where they bent over the ledge.

"It's too hard!" she called. "Let's rope down!"

But by then it was too late, and she knew it and held her breath. He was reaching higher now up into the crack, trying to get his fingers into it, but it was still too narrow and his right leg had begun to shake, slowly at first, then rapidly. She squinted up. *Oh God,* she thought, knowing he was in trouble, feeling a desperate sense of how small she was compared to everything around her.

Then, suddenly, she heard him cry out and saw him fall.

She bent the rope around her waist, felt nothing at first, then a stunning, lifting explosion of force that picked her up and slammed her back against the cliff, and she felt the rope burning hot through her gloved hands and across her back, twisting her sideways into a half crouched position; and she heard herself scream, and held the rope tightly against the searing pain until it stopped running at last and everything around the cliff was quiet again except for a whisper of breeze.

"*Gabe!*" she called. She tried to stand straight, but the length of webbing he had used to secure her to the ledge kept her from doing that, and the muscles in her back and legs, twisted unnaturally as they were, had already begun to knot into spasms. "*Gabe!*" she called. "*Help me!*"

There was no reply, only his dead weight on the rope and a terrible feeling of tension as if at any moment, from the stress it was under, the rope might snap. She felt a rush of panic, closed her eyes until the brunt of it had passed. Finally, she made herself look up.

From where she held it, the rope still ran in a sharp diagonal forty feet up to the small chock and sling that had stopped Gabe's fall, and from there twenty feet straight down now to the place where he hung motionless from it. He was facing out from the cliff. She could see a gash on the side of his forehead, and blood – a lot of blood it seemed – and the rope which had been knotted around his waist was now up under his arms.

"Gabe, can you hear me?" she said, her voice so slight she knew he couldn't hear, couldn't have heard in any case. "I'm going to lower you. Going to try."

She did that, lowering him what seemed an inch at a time, standing in her painful half crouched position, letting the rope run a little, stopping when it began to burn, then letting it run again. When at last he was lying on the ledge, she felt a sudden welling of tears from the relief that was, and she untied herself from the anchor webbing and went to kneel beside him, staying as close as she could to the wall.

"*Oh Gabe*," she whispered. "*Oh God, Gabe.*" He seemed like a stranger, someone she hardly knew lying helpless this way. His face, which had been deeply tanned, was sallow now. The area around the gash on his forehead had begun to swell, the gash itself seeped blood the same red color as the rope. Tentatively, she touched his throat, felt a faint pulse, saw the shallow rise and fall of his chest. He was badly hurt. Somehow, she was going to have to help.

Moving very carefully, she got the first-aid kit from the pack, cleaned and bandaged his head as best she could. Then she reknotted the rope at his waist and used it to secure him to the ledge so he would not be in danger should he suddenly come to. As she did these things she felt numb, as if she was standing aside and watching someone else do them. Gabe sighed. Small flecks of saliva collected along his lip. She spoke to him. He did not reply.

For a while after that she tried calling for help, but it was four miles from the ledge to the lake, and nothing but forest in between, and nobody answered her call except some crows that hawked and cried up out of the trees and glided like bats below the cliff. It was two o'clock. The sun, she knew, would set at eight.

She sat down, feeling frightened and alone, and sorry for Gabe who lay breathing quietly by her side, and angry too. He had always been so sure of himself, always impatient whenever, out of her natural caution, she would ask, What do I do if this happens? Or that?

You worry too much, he liked to say. *Leave the driving to me.* And that was exactly what she had done, and her awareness of it made her as angry as anything else.

There was no food in the pack, less than half a canteen of water. No matches. No flashlight. No extra clothes. None of the things she knew now they should have thought to bring. She had stuck the first-aid kit in at the last moment, remembered now that Gabe had been amused. She put her hands to her face, remembered too how his arms had felt around her on this same ledge when they had had their lunch, and how he had tossed grapes into the air, and how invulnerable he had seemed.

"I love you," she whispered.

He did not reply.

She took his hand in hers. Already his blood had begun to seep through the bandage she had made.

She would have to get help somehow, get off the cliff, but it seemed an impossible thing to do. She knew from their practice sessions that climbing down was much harder than climbing up; and though Gabe had given her a lesson in how to descend on the rope, he had not shown her how to set up the maneuver or even what equipment to use. He had always taken care of everything, in his quick sure way.

And he had been so *close,* she thought. Not ten feet from the top of the cliff.

She squinted up. The rope was still tied to her waist, still ran forty feet up to the lone chock and sling that had stopped his fall. From there it came down to the place where she had secured it to the ledge. The remainder of the cliff was a mass of gray granite that rounded toward the sky. The sun beat warmly against it, and the sky itself was clear and blue. A game trail wound down the back side of the mountain, a simple walk Gabe had said.

So close.

She stood up, trying to remember how it had gone for him before he had reached the bad place. Not so hard, she thought, because he had gone so high above the ledge before bothering to protect himself with that single chock and sling. The key to the bad place had been the final crack which had been too thin to take his hands, but might not be too thin to take hers. He had told her repeatedly that she was good, had seemed to mean it. Twice during their practice climbs she had managed to balance her way over some small holds that he had missed. She remembered his saying, *"Hey! You're not supposed to do that! You're making me look bad!"*

She decided finally that she would try climbing up. Of the chances she had, she thought this was best. She told herself she would only go as far as it was reasonably easy for her to go, that she would simply look things over. If it should get too hard, she would manage one way or another to climb back down to the ledge. Maybe she would be able to see something that he, in his impatience to be off the wall, had not seen.

The rock was steep, and warm under her hands. She moved carefully up from hold to hold, planning each move before she made it. At intervals, when she could, she reknotted the rope at her waist to keep too much slack from developing between her and the chock and sling above. This gave her a feeling of security, as if Gabe were up there as usual, taking in the rope as she climbed toward him, telling her not to worry, that she was doing fine, that he would stop her easily if she should start to fall.

But there was a coppery taste in her mouth and an overall sense of fear which increased with the beating of her heart now as she climbed higher and higher above the ledge. Fifteen feet. Twenty. Twenty-five. Her hands got slippery; she wiped them on her shorts. Perspiration began to sting her eyes. She tried to think of nothing except how she was going to move safely and efficiently up from one set of holds to the next, but the higher she went the more she began to be sure she had made a mistake and that it had been foolish of her to suppose she might manage something Gabe himself had not been able to do.

The breeze puffed up, blew wisps of her hair, then died. At the edge of her vision she could see him lying motionless on the ledge below, and below that the terrible long distance to the ground; and her stomach clenched suddenly, and she felt a dizzying surge.

God help me out of this, she thought.

At thirty-five feet above the ledge, she stopped to rest on some sizeable holds. She could see the chock and sling now, just above her. The chock was a small wedge of metal, with holes through its center, which Gabe had jammed into a crack in the rock. The sling was a loop of line that ran through the holes in the chock and hung down from the crack. The climbing rope was attached to the sling by an aluminum snap link about the size of a coaster. It all looked much too flimsy to have stopped someone the size of Gabe falling. She closed her eyes.

She could hear him talking to her, just as if he were here. *You're doing fine. Don't think about the distance to the ground— that doesn't matter. Just think about your holds. Try not to move more than one hand or foot at a time. Keep three solid points of contact with the rock. If you do come off, no problem: I'll have you stopped before you know it.*

And she had come off, too. Several times, before she had begun to get the hang of it.

She wiped her forehead, began to climb again. She climbed up slowly to the chock and sling, and then slowly and carefully above that until she came near the place where Gabe had been standing when he fell. Here, she could see a spot of lighter gray on the wall, as if one of his footholds had broken from under him, a small projection of rock, perhaps, that had been too fragile to support his weight as he had tried to move up into that final crack. Ten feet beyond her reach, the top of the cliff rounded toward the sky.

So close. And nothing left in her now of the idea of climbing back down to the ledge. She was going to finish. She had to.

The crack was there, like a door slightly ajar. She started to move toward it, felt a sudden tug at her waist, realized there was no more slack in the rope between her and the place where she had secured it to the ledge. She would have to untie now, haul up some slack from the free end, retie again.

She wished she had thought of this sooner. Below the chock and sling her holds had been fair-sized and comfortable. Now they were quite small, and the cliff so steep she felt as if it were a hand pushing her back and away.

She began to work the knot loose at her waist. It seemed to take a long time, but at last it came free and she hauled up some slack and tied in again. She wasn't sure how much good the rope would do her if she fell, but she felt better knowing it was there, knowing there was something, at least, that might keep her from falling all the way to the ground.

I can do this, she thought, *I've got to.*

The breeze had freshened now; she felt it as a coolness along her legs and arms. She inched up to the place where Gabe had fallen and finding her own small holds and holding her breath she inched past that place until she could reach the crack. It took the tips of her fingers at first, then, as she moved gingerly up from one hold to the next, it began to take all of her hand. The crack felt cool to her touch. She was pressed so close to the wall now she could smell the flinty smell of the rock and feel its rough texture against her cheek. On the narrow ledge below, Gabe lay inert, like a small rag doll in the place where she had left him. Her footholds now were the size of wine corks. She stood poised on them over 350 feet above the ground.

Catching her lip between her teeth, telling herself she could do this thing she had to do, she moved up. Another inch. Another foot. Her heartbeat had risen until she could hear it like the ticking of her father's mantel clock. Gnats sang in the air around her. She brushed them away from her eyes. Perspiration ran in cold runnels down the backs of her legs. She moved up. Another inch, and then another. The crack had begun to widen. She used it for her hands and found small holds on either side to place her feet. She had climbed now very close to the top of the cliff. It lay a little way beyond her reach, and she wanted more than anything she had ever wanted in her life to climb quickly and be off, but knew she must not.

She made herself stop for a minute and look things over before going on. The crack had continued to widen as it neared the top of the cliff, and she thought it might be wide enough just above the place where she stood to take the toe of her boot. She saw she was going to have to reach quite far and she did that with her right foot, bringing it awkwardly up until she got it into the crack. This put her into a position too uncomfortable to hold for long, and she took a deep breath and began to move up. She was halfway up when she felt the rope tug sharply at her waist again, and realized too late she had not allowed enough slack, and knew she was going to fall. *"Gabe!"* she screamed, clawing at the knot with one hand, holding herself desperately to the cliff with the other while the echo of her cry came back from the emptiness below: *Gabe! Gabe! Gabe!*

She tore at the knot. Her nail bent and broke. She bit

through her lip, tasted blood. The knot wouldn't loosen in spite of her efforts, and then did at last, and she felt the rope fall away with a whirring sound behind her, and she was without protection, hanging at near arm's length from the crack, with her boot jammed awkwardly high.

Oh God, she thought. *God . . . .*

Half blind with perspiration, she searched with her left foot for something that would hold her. Her body swayed with the motion of her leg, and her arm felt as if it would tear from its socket, as if she had to let go and might have in another half moment if her scrabbling left foot hadn't caught at last on a small rock nubbin big enough to balance up slowly slowly until she had both hands in the crack and all of her weight finally on her jammed right foot.

She closed her eyes, trembling, trying to breathe. The top of the cliff was in reach. She waited until she could, and then she finished the climb in three moves. When she was finally on top, and well back from the edge, she lay down on the warm rock surface and held herself tightly and cried.

The game trail was there, as Gabe had said it would be, winding down the far side of the mountain. She took it quickly, but carefully too; and when it joined the easier path that led through the forest to the lake, she began to run and jog and run again, twisting her ankle painfully once, the mosquitoes rising terribly around her whenever she slowed, her vision blurred by her tears, her breath sharp in her throat.

It was late afternoon when she finally reached the cottage. She called the local sheriff and explained what had happened. She was urgent and precise. The sheriff told her he knew the location of the cliff, that a team of rescuers would be formed and sent out at once. He said she should wait where she was for him to call, which he would do as soon as he had any word. She told him she'd feel better if she could go with the rescuers, but he said no, that she would help most by staying where she was, and so she did.

For a while, she sat by the phone, wanting desperately to call someone, to talk, but afraid to tie up the line, afraid to say to the person she might call: *He was alive when I left him, but that was hours ago. . . .*

The ankle she had twisted had begun to throb. There were abrasions on her hands and arms, and she was covered with dirt and felt a soreness in her shoulder that seemed to penetrate the bone. She decided finally it would be all right to take a shower, and she did that, standing tiredly under the drive of the showerhead, the door to the bathroom open so she wouldn't miss the phone if it rang. Gabe's shave kit was on the hamper, open and smelling of his particular cologne which she had always liked. The kit itself was handcrafted of leather, and before she left the room, she zipped it shut.

It won't be the same, she thought. *When we see each other again. If we do. . . .*

The thought had come to her fleetingly, and she did not pursue it.

There was casserole left from the supper she had fixed for the two of them the night before. She warmed some, but had no appetite, and though she made a stiff drink to take with her onto the screen porch, she only sipped at it, and gazed across the lake in the direction of the cliff where people she did not know were on their way to help her fiancé who had climbed to a high place and who had fallen and been hurt.

Then at last, how much later she could not have said, the phone finally rang and she hurried back into the cottage and snatched up the receiver, pressing it to her ear.

"Yes?" she said.

"He's off the mountain," the sheriff said. "They've got him over at County Hospital. . . ."

"Is he. . ." she started to say.

"Pretty banged up," the sheriff continued. "But the doctors say he's going to recover."

"Thank God," she said.

"Have you got a car?" the sheriff asked.

"Yes," she said.

"He'll need his personal things."

"I'll bring them," she said.

As she hung up the phone, the thought came to her again — sharper this time — that no matter how fully he recovered the two of them would never again be quite the same as they had been before his fall. They would be starting from a different point than the one they had reached on that high ledge at lunchtime today, when she had been so fearful of the climb, and he had grinned and had tossed grapes into his mouth.

Quickly, she began packing up his things.

We can deal with the changes when we have to, she thought.

She had taken her engagement ring off before the climb, and put it for safekeeping in the zipper pocket of her shorts. Now as she prepared to leave the cottage, she took it out and slipped it back on her finger, clenching her hand.

We can deal with the changes when we have to, she thought.

As she left the cottage the surface of the lake was flat, the color of tangerines now from the last of the sun.

In 1962 I climbed Shiprock, a 1700-foot volcanic monolith that rises dramatically from the desert floor on a Navajo Indian Reservation in the northwest corner of New Mexico. (The rock, I am told, is sacred to the Navajos, and has since been closed to climbers.)

It was for me a long, tiring climb (we began at dawn, finished at dusk), spectacularly exposed at times; and if I had not been lucky enough to have been climbing with Dave Rearick, I would not have made it to the top. Dave, who had done the first ascent of the Long's Peak Diamond, was in good spirits on the day of our Shiprock climb. He cheerfully free-climbed the aid pitches, then gave me a tight rope. The wind was blowing hard when we got to the top. The actual summit of Shiprock is about the size of a card table, and there is over a thousand-foot vertical drop off one side. Dave hopped right up there, admired the view, then came down so I could go up. I told him that in light of the gale that was blowing I thought I would settle for just reaching up and touching the summit, which I did. Dave got a big kick out of this. As soon as I had finished touching the summit, he hopped back up there, unroped, and did a handstand.

I used many of the details of the setting of Shiprock (but not of the climb itself) in "The Devil's Thumb."

Written: Phoenix, Arizona; Winter, 1965
First Published: *Phoenix Point West,* October, 1965
Reprinted: *Literary Cavalcade* (Scholastic Magazines), December, 1970
Order and Diversity: The Craft of Prose (John Wiley Publishers), 1973
Traits & Topics: An Anthology of Short Stories (Scott, Foresman and Company), 1976

THE DEVIL'S THUMB

Past midnight, Meyer woke again to the noise of the bat-like birds that shot past the narrow ledge, their high-pitched sounds like rushing pinwheels. He had fallen forward in the ropes that held him in a seated position so that his upper body now hung over the ledge, and when he opened his eyes he saw the desert floor 800 feet below him and the orange smudges that were the spectators' fires. Across the desert, the moon lay its imperfect light on the dark basalt mountains to the east, and the night sky was light and marked with gauzy streaks of cloud.

Meyer eased himself back until all his weight was on the ledge, his back resting on the wall of rock behind him. He saw that Devar had not moved. The older man sat five feet away, tied in to the same narrow ledge, his back straight and stiff against the wall, his eyes open, his teeth clamped tightly on the stem of his unlit pipe. Meyer could smell the whiskey, and in Devar's gaunt face, in the arched bone of his nose and white unblinking eyes, he saw again the signs of sorrow and what he thought now was some kind of madness.

"We can climb soon," he said.

The older man nodded, but did not answer.

"I wish we could start now," Meyer said. "I feel good; I've slept enough."

The birds rushed by again and a gust of wind brightened the fires far below the ledge. Meyer guessed there were a hundred people down there, asleep in their trucks and tents. They had come to see Devar climb the Devil's Thumb which, if he made it, would be one of the really great climbs of his long career. They had not come to see Meyer who was young and not yet well known; but he knew he could climb well and he wished more than anything that just once Devar would give him the lead.

He glanced to his left and saw the older man, his mournful and whiskered face bold in the half light of the moon. Funny duck that Devar. He climbed well enough, but he had brought more whiskey than water and he never talked. The tremendous enthusiasm Meyer had felt when Devar had written him and asked him to second this climb had long since faded to disappointment. Meyer knew what a hero should be, and the old man did not measure up. He had no idea how Devar had chosen him from all the promising young climbers in Colorado, but he already wished it had not happened. There was no excitement in following in the wake of this unapproachable veteran.

It was their third night on the Thumb, and in three days climbing from dawn until dusk they had made 800 feet. Above, the pinnacle rose 300 feet more. It was the highest unclimbed tower left in the southwest and of the many climbers who had tried to make the first ascent only two others had gone higher than this, and they had fallen to death from the Finger Traverse which crossed the rock 100 feet above Meyer's head. He squinted down and saw moonlight reflected from the quilted panels of a camper truck far below him, its dimensions toylike in the distance. The birds shot by the ledge and the wind moved Devar's parka, making it flap like a window shade on a breezy summer night. Before long, the sun would begin to rise and the two men would resume the climb. Meyer thought of this impatiently and made up dreams of what he would do if Devar gave up the lead. Before many minutes passed, he had fallen against the ropes, asleep.

Three hours later, when it was still night, the older man shook him awake. He had set their breakfast between them on the ledge, pemmican and jerky, a mix of brown sugar and raisins, and one of the pint-sized flasks of water. They ate in silence, Meyer eating rapidly, eager to be finished, Devar eating slowly, as if by habit. When they were done, Meyer stuffed the empty flask and the plastic bags that had held the food into a crack at the seam where the ledge met the wall. He then filled a small climbing pack with food, water, and a first-aid kit; they would leave their two large packs on this ledge to pick up on their descent. When Meyer finished, the two men made ready to climb.

Meyer said, "Today we'll be on the summit."

Devar did not answer.

When their preparations were over, Devar stood ten feet to the right of Meyer, facing the rock. In the rock, midway between them at a height of five feet above the ledge, was the piton Devar had been anchored to during the night. It was a six-inch Austrian angle piton driven to its ring in a tight horizontal crack. An aluminum carabiner was snapped to the ring, but Devar was no longer tied to it. One end of a 150-foot nylon rope was passed three times around his waist and tied with a bowline knot. The rope went from his waist freely through the carabiner to Meyer. Meyer now stood on the ledge, still tied to his own piton. He faced Devar and held the rope so that it passed from his left hand across his back to his right hand and from there to the remaining rope which was coiled on the ledge at his feet. He wore gloves and his attitude was that of a man holding the reins of a horse. Eight hundred feet below him he could see the toylike autos and trucks and the shreds of smoke above the fires. He could not yet see the sun that was coming up in back of the black mountains, but the sky was lightening and the stars were fading and when the wind blew, it was warm and carried fragments of conversation from the people who were up and starting their breakfasts.

The itch to trade places with Devar burned hotly in Meyer, the sureness that he could climb as well as the older man whose name was known to every climber in the country, that given the chance he could lead the Thumb and be the first ever to stand on its summit.

"I'm ready," Devar said.

"Climb," Meyer answered.

Devar began. The first 20 feet were easy. He climbed smoothly and swiftly, and Meyer paid out the rope. Twenty feet above the ledge, the angle of rock steepened to 85 degrees and the system of cracks that Devar was following began to thin out, providing him with fewer and less adequate holds. He stopped. Circling his body from right shoulder to left hip was a short length of rope to which were clipped two dozen carabiners, and hanging from each carabiner were one or two pitons of different shape and size. Devar unclipped one piton. It looked like a tapering steel tent peg with an eye drilled through the wide end. He placed it part way into a thin vertical crack in the rock above his left shoulder and then, removing a hammer from a leather loop on his belt, he drove the piton into the crack until only the eye was showing. Then he snapped a carabiner through the eye. The carabiner was aluminum and looked like a link from a large chain except that it had a spring gate which could be pressed open and snapped shut.

Devar clipped his rope into the carabiner so that when he climbed, the rope would run freely up from the ledge through the carabiner to his waist. If he fell, Meyer would hold the rope, and the piton, if it stayed in the crack, would stop the fall.

"How is it?" Meyer shouted.

"All right," Devar said.

Devar began climbing again. The angle of rock rose to 90 degrees. In ten feet, he drove another piton. Meyer could hear the sound coming down through the rock, the rising metallic pitch that sounded like a spike being driven into green wood and meant the piton was tight in the crack. He knew that for himself there was nothing to equal leading a high and difficult pitch, finding a workable route and setting the pitons well. Belaying the leader was second best, like paddling bow in a canoe, or flying a plane from the co-pilot's seat. Meyer flexed his hands and leaned against the rock with his left shoulder.

Now the rope ran up from the ledge freely through the first carabiner and freely through the second to Devar's waist. Meyer watched, working the rope. Devar moved up slowly toward the traverse. Over the black mountains, the sun rose huge and orange and out of all proportion to the sky. On the desert, 800 feet below Meyer's right foot, he saw figures begin to move, dark gesticulating specks against the yellow earth. Whereas in the beginning he had found it necessary to pay out the rope swiftly to keep up with Devar, he now paid it out very slowly.

As Devar inched up toward the traverse, he drove in more pitons and clipped in to them. Once, he was on the same holds for twenty minutes, and when he finally moved up he moved up less than a foot and it was another twenty minutes before he moved again. Meyer felt the wind warm against his face. On the desert floor, he saw the specks move, together and away from each other, into and out of cars, toward and away from the base of the rock. He knew that many of them had binoculars and were watching Devar as he moved up toward the traverse. He wondered whether he could lead the pitch as well as the older man, and whether he could lead it better. The sun rose steadily into the sky, growing smaller and hotter. Devar's sweat fell 80 feet to the ledge where Meyer stood paying out the rope which now ran freely up through nine carabiners to Devar's waist. The drops of sweat evaporated on the warm rock at his feet. One day, he thought, I will lead and the crowds will be there and someone else will follow.

In two and one half hours the older man had reached a small ledge just below the start of the traverse, had driven an anchor piton and had tied himself to it with a short length of rope. He stood on the ledge, facing out, and Meyer heard him call "Off belay."

Standing on the bivouac ledge, Meyer untied from his anchor piton. Then, with his hammer, he struck the head of the piton back and forth and up and down until it was loose in the crack, and then he gripped the carabiner and shook it until he was able to pull the piton from the crack. He clipped the carabiner and piton to a short loop of rope that hung from his shoulder, and stepped along the ledge to Devar's original piton which he also knocked out of the crack. As he did these things, Devar took up the rope so there was no slack between the two men.

"Ready to climb," Meyer called.

"Climb," Devar answered.

The two men were joined by the long rope. It was tied around Meyer's waist and went from there freely up through the series of carabiners to the ledge, 100 feet above, where Devar held it across his back and in his left and right hands, taking in the slack as Meyer climbed. Meyer felt sun on his back and the rock warm and grainy under his hands. When he reached Devar's first piton, he stood balanced on small holds and knocked the piton loose, drawing it out of the crack and clipping it to the short rope looped over his shoulder. When he looked up, he could see the worn cleated soles of Devar's climbing shoes where they extended beyond the thin ledge, and when he looked down beyond his own shoes he could see the desert 820 feet below and the specks of people moving around, and the larger objects that were the cars and trucks. He felt supremely confident and his irritation at being second on the rope almost disappeared in the joy of climbing up the steep and difficult pitch.

As he climbed up toward Devar, he removed the pitons and carabiners that the older man had placed. He climbed much more swiftly than Devar had climbed. The rope ran straight from his waist up to the ledge where Devar held it, taking in the slack as Meyer moved up so that if Meyer came off his holds he would not fall but would hang by the rope until he regained his holds. As second, it was his job to remove all the pitons Devar had placed and to cover the route as quickly as possible. If a piton did not come out readily, he called for direct aid. Then Devar would take in all the slack until the rope was very tight between them and Meyer would lean back on the rope with his feet braced on the wall, the way a window washer leans against a safety belt, both hands free to work the piton.

Forty minutes after he began climbing, he reached the ledge where Devar stood. He had climbed the pitch quickly, but he had also evaluated the difficulty of each move and the adequacy of the pitons Devar had set. He rated the pitch at 5.9 by the decimal system scale, which meant it was difficult in the extreme. He understood why so many men had turned back from the pitch and he was confident that if he had led it he would have made it and that he would have done it more quickly than Devar.

"You climbed that well," Devar said.

"Thanks, I was climbing second; it's not the same. You did the work."

Devar stood next to him on the ledge, his long face bristling with whiskers, sweat sparkling in the hollows of his eyes. He did not answer Meyer's compliment, and once again the younger man felt disappointment. Devar could not be reached. He was remote, isolated, uncommunicative. Meyer tried again.

"Now the traverse," he said. He could not hide his enthusiasm; the traverse was all that stood between them and the summit. That the first two men who tried to cross it had been killed meant only that they had been unlucky.

Again, Devar did not respond. They changed the belay. Meyer stood tied in to the anchor piton and faced Devar. Devar, no longer tied in to the anchor piton but still tied to the end of the 150-foot rope, moved to the end of the ledge and looked up at the Finger Traverse. It was a much thinner ledge,

60 feet long and tapered like a pool cue. The wide end was just above Devar's head and the thin end was 60 feet to his left. There, another big ledge began at the level of the one on which he now stood. It was that opposing ledge that Devar would have to reach, and he could do so only by swinging along the traverse.

"I'm ready," Devar said.

"Climb," Meyer said.

Devar selected a piton and held it between his teeth, and he put his hammer in the breast pocket of his parka. Then he reached up and gripped the ledge and swung out so that he hung by his fingers, 900 feet above the ground. Moving swiftly, he slid his left hand as far as he could reach to the left, and then slid his right hand to meet it. He moved this way for 30 feet and then he stopped. Hanging by the fingers of his left hand, he took the piton he had clenched in his teeth and forced it by hand into a crack just below the traverse ledge. When it was wedged, he took out his hammer and drove the piton tightly into the crack and clipped a carabiner to it. Then, still hanging by the fingers of his left hand, he clipped the climbing rope into the carabiner and called for direct aid. Meyer took in the rope, keeping it very tight, and Devar, with both hands now on the traverse ledge, pulled himself up until the knot at his waist was close to the carabiner. Then he let go and hung from the piton.

Meyer watched him. The older man opened and closed his hands, working the cramps out of them. His eyes were closed and when he opened them he looked across the 30 feet left of the traverse and closed his eyes again. Meyer stood, holding the rope tightly. Nine hundred feet below the edge of his left shoe, he could see the specks grouped now and motionless on the desert floor. He wanted Devar to succeed on the traverse simply because he would never wish for another man's failure. But short of this, he would have given anything to be in the older man's place.

They had been on the wall four days, each day hotter than the last. Now the sun beat against the rock and the heat was terrible. Devar hung from the piton, his arms limp at his sides, his eyes closed. Meyer waited, the rope tight in his hands and across his back, passing over the short rope that tied him to the wall and crossing the traverse to Devar. When the wind blew, it was warm and sometimes carried voices although Meyer could not distinguish the words. He knew Devar had been right to drive the piton. The other man who had tried the traverse had tried to go all the way to the far ledge and gotten 45 feet across and had fallen. The force of that fall had torn his belayer from the rock. It was right to put the piton in midway on the traverse, but Meyer knew what it had taken, like doing a chin-up with the fingers of one hand and hanging a full minute, maybe longer. Admiration for Devar's strength and skill mingled with his disappointment in the man.

When Devar reached up and gripped the traverse ledge, he called "Climbing." Meyer relaxed his hold on the rope and paid out slack to Devar. Devar swung along the ledge by his fingertips, his feet scraping against the wall, dislodging grit and chips of rock that drifted down 900 feet like pieces of confetti. Meyer let out the rope. His heart was pumping and he mumbled encouragement to the older man. Devar got 15 feet beyond the piton he had driven below the center of the traverse. Then he paused, scraping the narrowing ledge with the nails of his left hand, trying to get a decent hold. His movements were rapid, those of a man who is counting his time in seconds. Finally he found a hold and hung from it by the first joints of the fingers of his left hand and brought his right hand to meet his left. He hung that way for a few seconds, 900 feet above the desert, his hands together and at arms length above his head, his feet dangling. Then he glanced at Meyer and said, "I'm going to fall."

Meyer nodded and braced himself on his ledge. When Devar fell, he fell like a sack of wheat, straight down until his weight hit the piton, and then he swung across the wall like the pendulum of a clock. Meyer let the rope run a few feet to soften the impact of the fall and brought him to a gradual stop. Devar swung back and forth in long arcs, pushing himself away from the wall with his hand until he gradually slowed and came to a stop, hanging like a plumb weight 20 feet below the traverse piton.

Meyer shouted, "You're a lousy bird!" He was relieved that the older man was safe.

Devar looked up. There was no fear in his expression, but there was irritation. Above him, the wall was smooth, but running diagonally from where he hung to the ledge where Meyer stood was a series of cracks and small nubbins of rock. Devar found holds and began to climb toward Meyer. Meyer worked the rope as Devar climbed up. It took the older man 20 minutes to reach the ledge. When he did, the rope was running from Meyer, across the traverse to the piton, and back to Devar.

"I'll have to rest," Devar said.

Meyer nodded. From the small climbing pack he got out some chocolate and a water flask, and Devar ate and drank. The sky was bright and cloudless and waves of heat shimmered over the desert so that the outlines of the basalt mountains were indistinct and had the appearance of something seen in a mirage. Nine hundred vertical feet below the ledge, the black ciphers waited motionless for Devar to try again.

When he did, he moved swiftly and passed the traverse piton and went 20 feet beyond it before he fell. This time he fell suddenly, without warning Meyer, dropping again like a sack of wheat and penduluming across the wall. The rope scorched Meyer's gloves as he let it run and slowed it down and braked it. This time it took Devar 30 minutes to regain the ledge where Meyer stood. His hands were bleeding. Meyer looked away from him; he did not want to see the old man's eyes.

Then Devar said, "I'm ready."

Hanging by his fingers, he swung across the traverse, past the piton, 15 feet, 20 feet, until he was five feet from the opposing ledge. For a few seconds he hung there, unable to go further, and watched fiercely as his fingers uncurled and began to slip from the ledge. Then he fell again. This time he hung from the rope a long while, and when he began climbing it took him 40 minutes to reach the ledge where Meyer stood. When he reached the ledge he did not say anything for a while. His hands were raw and bleeding, his face was cut and his parka was torn below the left shoulder.

"I don't think I can go again," he said finally.

Meyer felt suddenly helpless and, because he did not know what else to do, he began talking.

"It looks like it will have to be climbed," he said. "As much as we can see of the wall below the traverse, there are small nicks and nubbins, not much, but enough to take the edge of a klettershoe. Suppose a man were to go hand over hand to the piton and then rest on direct aid, not a little while but for a long time, and while he was resting he could study the wall from the piton to the far ledge. It's only 30 feet; a few key holds, especially in the last five feet, would take stress off the hands and arms. It might go that way."

Meyer talked on, and while he talked he busied himself with the canteen and chocolate, preparing a snack for the older man. He was upset and didn't know why, and talking was all he could think of to do.

"I think it will go," he said. "You almost had it the last time, five feet more, but you couldn't find anything for your feet." He glanced down at Devar's feet and saw again that the man's shoes were worn. "Your boots are pretty old, the edges are rounded and the soles are probably getting soft. You could wear mine, they may be a little big, but we could wrap your feet with cloth." He steadied himself on the thin ledge and, using a small pocket knife, he cut a sleeve off his own shirt, tore it in two pieces, and put the cloth in his teeth. Then he raised one foot and carefully untied his shoelace. Devar watched him, breathing more easily now, the sweat bright in the hollows of his eyes. "You'll have to take yours off," Meyer said. "We'll trade one at a time."

Devar removed one boot, wrapped his foot with the half sleeve that Meyer gave him, and put on Meyer's shoe, tying the laces very tight.

"How does it feel?" Meyer asked.

The older man moved his foot beyond the ledge until only a quarter of an inch of the sole touched the rock; then he let it take his weight. "Good," he said.

When they completed the exchange of shoes, Devar rested 30 more minutes and then moved out on the traverse. Hand over hand, he crossed easily to the piton, pulled himself up and called for direct aid. Meyer took in all the slack and held the rope hard against his back. Devar let go of the traverse ledge and hung from the piton. He rested for 15 minutes, and while he rested he studied the wall below the opposing ledge. Finally, Meyer heard his call that he was ready to climb.

He moved swiftly across the remaining section of the traverse until he was five feet from the opposing ledge. Meyer paid out the rope, his teeth clenched, his heart beating very hard, his eyes fastened on the man who hung by his hands, 900 feet above the desert.

Slowly, Devar moved his right foot to a hold which must have been very small, and Meyer saw that it took part of his weight. The sun beat down, and sweat glistened from Devar's face and from the corded muscles of his forearms, and spread out in stains along the side of his parka. Again slowly, he moved his left foot until it found a hold, and he let it take part of his weight. He was now spread-eagled on the wall, holding on with the tips of his fingers and a fraction of the sole of each shoe.

He lay his cheek against the rock. Meyer watched him. He knew the spectators were watching, too, wondering whether the old man would make it or not.

Five feet to the left of Devar's left foot, the broad ledge lay hot in the bright sun, a ledge on which no man had ever stood. The next move was critical; Meyer knew if Devar fell again he would be finished. He held the rope tightly in both hands and felt the tips of his fingers pulse, and it was as if the rope carried his own blood to the older man.

When Devar moved again, he moved his right hand along the traverse ledge until it reached his left, and he tensed the fingers of both hands. Then, moving swiftly, he hung from his fingers and raised his left foot from its hold and let his right foot come to it. Then, easing part of his weight onto his right foot, he moved his left hand as far as he could and found a hold. For a moment he wavered, and then he brought his right hand to his left and, stretching as far as he could with his left foot, he reached the broad ledge and stepped lightly on to it, swinging by his hands across the remaining gulf.

Meyer made no gesture or sound, but smiled as he held the rope; and he felt the wind blow up the face and heard the sounds of the people shouting. Above Devar's ledge, a series of wide cracks and shelves went to the summit of the Thumb; the difficult moves were over. The older man climbed up 50 feet above the traverse so Meyer would have a safe belay. He anchored himself to a comfortable ledge and took in the slack. Meyer heard his call to climb.

Before climbing, Meyer looked east across the desert to the black mountains and then straight down almost a thousand feet and saw the people moving on the sand; and it occured to him what it might be like to reach the end of a long career, a time which he could only vaguely imagine when he too might become uncommunicative and bring whiskey and sit sleepless through the long nights, bivouacked on a high wall.

Then, in Devar's old shoes, which were very tight for him, he crossed the traverse easily and well.

I had a student at Northeastern University who came to me once after class (in 1971 when the war between the sexes was running at a fever pitch) and asked me if I was familiar with the stories in Playboy *magazine. I had to admit I wasn't. He said he thought the stories were quite good and left me several recent issues of the magazine so I could judge for myself. I took these magazines home and studied them with a great deal of care. When I was through, I decided I was going to try and write a story for* Playboy.

I remember thinking that a story for Playboy *probably should have something to do with the relationship between a man and a woman, so I put that down — and, because a couple of my climbing stories had at that point done all right in the small magazine market, I decided the man and the woman I would write about would be climbers.*

I had had occasion once to camp for a couple of days in a cottonwood grove in Canyon de Chelly in eastern Arizona and had been pretty much struck dumb by the grandeur of the place — and of Spider Rock, a spectacular sandstone tower that rises vertically between the canyon walls. Canyon de Chelly became the inspiration for my setting.

Phil Fowler, an old climbing friend who lived in Laramie, Wyoming, had recently purchased a four-wheel-drive vehicle which he had christened "The Old Bull of the Woods." I borrowed this vehicle for my story and added the "Moose."

I have since puberty been an avid fan of Bluegrass music — particularly that of Lester Flatt, Earl Scruggs, and the Foggy Mountain Boys. I decided to have my protagonist be a good old boy from Texas who might be expected to share my taste in music. When I tried to hear my good old boy talk, the first thing he said to me was, "Howdy! Rat fan day fer a clam!"

When "The Old Bull Moose of the Woods" first appeared, in 1972, I received a report from a friend who was teaching a fiction writing seminar at the University of Chicago, that some of his women students had found the story to be "outrageously sexist."

I am still trying to understand that report.

Written: Bow Lake, Strafford, New Hampshire; Autumn, 1971

First Published: *Playboy*, July, 1972

Reprinted: *Playboy's Laughing Lovers* (Playboy Press), 1975

THE OLD BULL MOOSE
OF THE WOODS

GATE. Kachina Canyon, Arizona. Forty-foot aspen pole balanced on log fulcrum by 100-pound sack of meal. Gatehouse shaped like coffin on end containing one 150-year-old Indian chief. White shoulder-length hair under black Navajo hat, bleached denim, skin color of walnut, hollow cheeks, eyes locked in winter past, mouth sewed shut with a deer gut.

"Howdy!" Jay-D said.

Clipboard over door of Old Bull Moose. *Experience.* Jay-D filled it in. *Number in party. Name and address. Registration. Next of kin!!*

"Rat fan day!" Jay-D said.

Steel strongbox over door of Old Bull Moose, lid up, sign taped there: $100 – IN ADVANCE. "Yessir, rat fan!" C-note plucked from sweatband of bush hat, held for moribund chief to see, dropped into steel box, BANG! "Fella could lose his fingers," Jay-D said.

Clipboard, strongbox tucked into coffin. One 40-foot aspen so neatly balanced it could be raised and lowered by the oldest man alive on the desert reservations. Jay-D idled under the gate. Uneasy. Question to ask, but how?

Wicker, Jay-D. Hero of piece. 21. Lubbock, Texas. Rover a birthday gift from his pappy ("Jest tell me whut yew want, boy!" Jay-D told him). Only child. Bleached blond hair, blue eyes ("Handsome Daddy," the *Lubbock Annual* said. "Ladies' Man." "Candy is dandy, but Wicker is quicker!"). Glen Campbell voice, hillbilly drawl, not as tall as would like to have been, 5' 10" with rock shoes on, red socks, high-cut dark leather climbing shorts (Austrian), bush hat with chin strap (Australian), no shirt, bodybuilder's physique, chiseled and planed, 16-inch arms, abdominals like briquettes, exposed surfaces tanned and haired, square white teeth.... Rising climber, Southwest. First ascents 26 pinnacles, New Mexico, Arizona, Utah. Cover story last month, *Texas Parade* (Question: What accounts for your success as a climber, Mr. Wicker? Answer: When Ah want somethin', Ah go fer it.). Wanted Cholla Rock, Kachina Canyon.

THE OLD BULL MOOSE OF THE WOODS. Words lettered in red on driver's door of black 1971 Rover. Rack of moose antlers (genuine) fitted forward on hood. Decals of Satan astride gold fork and phrase (get close if you want to read it) AH'M A HORNY DEVIL! Tape deck. Sixteen cassettes. Everything Lester Flatt and Earl Scruggs ever recorded *(You Are My Flower* just ending, *Salty Dog* about to begin). Indoor-outdoor red-pile carpet on floors, walnut dash and wheel, silver inlays, leather map pockets, air horn. . .climbing gear under neoprene tarp in back, 150-foot coils of red-and-white Perlon rope, bandoleers, *étriers,* swami belts, wedges and nuts, *pitons* and carabiners, enough for the Eiger North Wall, the best money could buy, $3,000,000 in the trust fund.... Jest tell me whut yew want, boy.

Cholla Rock. 860-foot red-stone pinnacle. Never been climbed. Sacred to Indians. But hard times in villages now, new generation. For $100, cash in advance. . .apply at gatehouse (story by Newhall, *Albuquerque News*). Wanted that rock, Jay-D Wicker, a long time. Feather in bush hat. April 1972. Clear day, bright sun, top down. 84 west-northwest from Lubbock. Interstate 40 (old 66!) west to Gallup. Then north on Indian roads, winter-cut, dust-dry. Fort Defiance. Sawmill. Chinle formation. Flocks of sheep led by belled goats. Tumbleweed, mesquite. . .Flatt and Scruggs. . .*(Cripple Creek)*. . . .

Too many winters in that old chief's eyes, like holes in a frozen lake. The mouth a three-quarter-inch seam between two empty cheeks and a pointed chin.

"This here's mah vee-hickle," Jay-D said. Patted walnut wheel. Saw movement in chief's eyes. "Got 'er all bored out, she'll do a hundred thirty on the flat . . . ." Words lettered in red on black finish. Chief close enough to read.

"Horny," he said. Voice came from last year. Very deep. Arm rose to point, motion smooth as gate rising. Grin spread seams of cheeks to leather lobes of ears. Gums revealed. Could bite bolt in two. "Horny-ho-ho."

"Dōgged!" Jay-D said. "Ah knew it!"

CHOLLA ROCK 6 MILES / CAMPGROUND 3 MILES / CLIMBERS REGISTER AND PAY FEE / CANYON FLOODED IN SPRING / CARRY OUT GARBAGE / NOTHING ELSE.

"Be seein' yah!"

(Goin' Down That Road, Feelin' Fine.)

Two miles into canyon before he saw girl ankle deep in flood, wading away from him, short pants, long legs, Kelty Pack bobbing red under late sun (*must* have heard Old Bull Moose whining behind her, Jay-D, Flatt and Scruggs, but never turned around).

"Dōgged," Jay-D said. Lit himself a Between-The-Acts, pushed bush hat back, edged up into corner between seat and door, brought the Rover up, idled alongside her, sighted down nose, squinted eyes. "Dōgged!" he said. Little cigar between his teeth.

No reply. Same steady pace, straight ahead, splashing through the flood. Long brown hair tied off with rubber band and hung along close side of face in mare's-tail. Good-looker. Built. 18. Jay-D idling alongside, eyes watering from smoke. Walked up out of flood onto stretch of sand past stand of cottonwood where birds sang old melody. What approach to take? Females delicate. Required special treatment. ("Yew got tew be subtul," his pappy said. "Yew wouldn't tickle yore nose with a fence post!") Decided to blow air horn. Reached out, touched lever. Horn had always been loud. Here in canyon, it was louder than any horn ever heard in life, four times as loud as horn on tandem ten-wheeler. Scared himself with it, by golly.

And the girl who had walked through the flood and across the sand without breaking stride or looking at him jumped one foot above the ground and let out shriek.

"Howdy, ma'am," Jay-D said.

Unshouldered Kelty Pack. Turned to face him. Down front of denim shirt two bands of sweat where padded straps had been. No underthings. Jay-D looked. Good tits. Mad as a hornet.

"You idiot!"

"Ma'am?"

"*What* do you think you are doing?"

"Well, now. . . ."

"Why are you doing this? What do you want?"

Jay-D tipped head, squinted eyes, moved cigar between teeth. "Ma'am?"

"Why are you following me? What do you want? Your truck is obscene!"

"*Whut?*" Jay-D hollering over Scruggs-plink and Flatt-twang. Turned stereo down. *(Hard Travelin.)*

"Ob," she said, "scene."

Jay-D nodded.

"Blatant and ludicrous."

"Yas, ma'am."

"Utterly without redeeming qualities. Patently ridiculous. Buffoonish. Obviously owned by a lout. Turn it around, please, and go back where you came from."

"Whee-oo!" Jay-D said.

Arms folded across front where he had been looking. Raised eyebrows thick, real; vein beating in center of forehead. "Have I made myself *quite* clear?"

"Ma'am, whut is a purty thang lak yew —"

"I am not the least bit interested," she said, "in your dull-witted assessment of me as a 'pretty thing.' "

"Sorry, ma'am."

"You *exude* male chauvinism."

"Ma'am?"

"Male," she said, "chauvinism." Picked up Kelty Pack. Shouldered it. Padded straps in place over sweat lines.

"Yew headin' that way?" Jay-D asked.

"Obviously."

"Campground's 'nuther mal. Rat proud tew give yew a lift. . . ."

"I do not want a lift, thank you."

"Tote yore freight fer yew. . . ."

"I am quite capable," she said, "of 'toting it' myself." Walked away from him, across what was left of sandy stretch, back into flood. Jay-D watched movement of shorts, heard feet splash above idle of Old Bull Moose. Patches of snow on canyon rim crimson in westering sun. Ejected cassette. Injected another. Lit fresh cigar. Drove on. When passing girl thigh deep in flood, smiled, tipped hat. *(The Last Public Hanging in Old West Virginia.)*

Question: What do you do, Mr. Wicker, when you reach, say, an unclimbable section of rock, something extremely difficult, impossible even? Answer: "There's more'n one way tew shuck corn."

Campground deserted. Maybe not for long. On to Cholla Rock. 800-foot red-stone rocket on 60-foot launching pad. Good crack system west side looked like a go. Jay-D so excited had to get out and pee. High ground on east side. Grove of cottonwood, room to park Old Bull Moose. Found surprise. Flag in clearing, hung from forked tree. Out to investigate. Jordan Marsh brassiere. 38-D. Claimed ground for Gerry mountain tent. Cerulean blue. Zipped shut. Jay-D scratched briquettes on either side of navel. "Dōgged," he said, with reverence. Unzipped tent fly. Looked in. Found another surprise.

In search of conquest, man lays plans, not willy-nilly. Jay-D collected wood for fire, kindled same inside circle of stones on high ground out of clearing not far from Old Bull Moose. Smoke rose into what was left of light of day. Swallows swooped from crags of Cholla to look in on new arrival. Water burbled on way to place where old chief stood by aspen gate. Coals snapped. Eastern walls of canyon turned color of blood. At last gleaming, coyote barked. Then reduction of perceivable things to six-foot diameter of fire's light. Soup was on. Honor the provider. Large aluminum pot. Odor of onions traceable in smoke drift. Not one but two cups. Not one but two spoons. Two forks, two knives, two plates. Dinty Moore's Beef Stew. Instant pudding. Stereo switched to portable batteries now *(Roll in My Sweet Baby's Arms, Cabin in the Pines, The Great Philadelphia Lawyer, Hot Corn, Cold Corn, The Wreck of the Old 97)*. Finally, unmistakably, a splashing in the flood. Jay-D, in orange Sierra jacket now, observable leaning against pack on high ground near fire. Legs stretched out. Bush hat low on brow.

"Howdy, ma'am!"

Six miles a far piece in daylight through flood carrying Kelty Pack. Perhaps too far, even in redeeming presence at trail's end of onion-scented smoke, reacquaintance, light, warmth, all the verities of home is where the hearth is. Onto high ground then and past our hero, straight ahead to clearing. Not a word. Not an eyeblink. "There yew go," Jay-D said. Got up slowly to follow. Butt sore from riding Old Moose over Indian roads. Rubbing glutei with flats of hands.

"Obviously, this is *not* going to be my day." Her welcome. Hands and knees on ground in grove now, trying to light fire. Match blowing out in breeze. Whisk of bats in air.

"Now, don't yew waste yore tam on that, yew swate thang,"

Jay-D said. "Ah got supper in the pot."

Stood up. Faced him.

"*What* did you say?"

"Ah said Ah got supper in the pot – soap, stew and butter-scotch. 'Nuff there fer two bulldōggers. Come on 'fore the varmints git it."

"I have no intention of eating with you," she said.

"Yew don't?"

"I certainly do not."

"Dinty Moore's stew, ma'am. Onion soap. . . ."

"I do not wish to hear about it."

Jay-D hooked thumbs in belt. Contemplated while she lit small propane lantern with frosted globe. Gentle light. Soft hiss.

"Ma'am," he said. "Have Ah offended yew?"

"Yes," she replied, "you most certainly have."

"Yew mane comin' up on yew the way Ah did and hittin' the horn lak that?"

Wince from the wench. "Believe me," she said, "that is only part of it."

"And do Ah take it yew thank mah vee-hickle is"– had to rustle up a word –"*over*done?"

"Your 'vee-hickle,' as you say, is obscene."

"Mah hort's in the rat place."

"Is it really?"

"Would Ah have cooked supper fer yew if it warn't? Would Ah?"

"Speaking frankly," she said, "I would be very much inclined to distrust you in all your endeavors."

"*Lord*," Jay-D said.

"Now will you please leave? I am tired and hungry, and I plan to be up very early in the morning. I would also appreciate it if you would turn down that, that —"

"Lester Flatt and Earl Scruggs, ma'am."

"Yes. That."

Finished talking, apparently. Hands and knees again. Up

to Jay-D to invest encounter with life. Bring things back from the edge.

"Which sad yew figger to clam?"

"*What* did you say?"

"Ah said, which sad yew figger to clam?" Nod of bush hat in direction of Cholla.

Bounced up. Looked at him closely. "How do you know I am going to climb anything?" Not to be answered. Texas thumbs hooked now in back flap pockets of Austrian shorts. "You looked in my tent, didn't you?" Taking the Fifth. "Didn't you?!"

"Well, yas, ma'am, Ah did."

"What *unmitigated* nerve!"

"Yas, ma'am, Ah can see it was *un*warranted."

Her hands on hips. Vein visible on temple. Sweet pulsing thing, carried blood from hort to haid. Glanced around grove. "And my brassiere. . . ."

"Thought it was a flag, ma'am. Attracted mah attention soon as Ah arrived."

"You are des*pic*able!"

Reflex shrug from Jay-D. Instincts honed since 14 suggest new tack is desirable.

"Yew ain't really about tew try and clam that pinnacule by yoreself, are yew?"

"Do you find that upsetting?"

"Ah jest don't thank a girl —"

"You don't."

"No, ma'am."

"You have a remarkable way of never disappointing me."

"Thank yew, ma'am. . . ."

"If you wait around until tomorrow – which I personally hope you do not – you may lose some of your feckless attitudes regarding what I imagine you refer to as 'the opposite sex.' "

"Ma'am, Ah'm not reckless."

"Feckless!"

"Yes, ma'am."

"Now, I am faced with an arduous climb. If you have no further recommendations. . . ."

"Ah got one."

"You do."

"Yes, ma'am. Ah'd recommend the west sad."

"You would."

"Yes, ma'am."

Moment of silence. Dawning of new light. Not from lantern.

"Oh, no," she said.

"Ma'am?"

"You're not. . . ."

"Why, shore! Ah come tew clammer her, too!"

Kachina Canyon. Dark as deep well. Cuticle moon. Night air in April skinbracer cool. Fire thump, stream burble, bat whisk, breeze rustle, frog rivet. Jay-D Wicker turned in. Old jungle hammock strung from one branch of moose antler across high ground to forked tree from which flag had been struck after sundown. Last cassette played out. Foggy Mountain Boys racked up for night after fourth encore of old favorite *(Po' Rebel Soldier / Long Way from Home)*.

"Hail," Jay-D said. Hands on stomach. Enough soup to float side-wheeler, enough stew and butterscotch to sink it. "Had mah smarts, Ah'd of waited till breakfast anyhow. Let her git used tew me. Come up on her slow."

Plan B. Rise early. Beans and bacon. Hot coffee. Some spiritual songs *(Joy Bells, Father's Table Grace, I Saw Mother with God Last Night)*. When time right, suggest two can do things easier than one. Strategy. ("Boy, Ah do wish yew'd use yore haid fer somethin' 'sads ah hatrack!") Subtul.

Coyotes on east rim kindled color of autumn leaves by first light of April sun, howling up an Indian from Lubbock, Texas. Stealthy. Cunning. Out to collect water in bush hat to keep from banging pot. Subtle son of his father creeping 60 yards downwind to fart ("Yew better go aisy on them banes, boy!") Banes in the pot. Bacon in the pan. Wake up Foggy Mountain Boys. Softly! Softly! Just a tad above the beat of a humming-bird's wing ("I'll be going to heaven sometime, sometime / I'll be going to heaven sometime. . . ."). Toward the perimeter. Hort on Sierra sleeve.

"Mornin', ma'am! Rat fan day fer a clam!"

Silence in the sacred grove. All flags struck. Cerulean fly zipped shut tighter than an old buck's mouth. Beauty sleeping.

"Ma'am?"

An answer. Not the stuff of dreams while hung between old antler and forked tree. Nor even virtue rewarded. But distant rising ring (ping-ping) of steel _piton_ going into crack in west face of Cholla Rock. Driven with resolution. Straight ahead.

"Dang it!" our hero cries. _"She left me at the gate!"_

Disengage subtleties. Engage action. Flush of temper, even. Sprint across high ground, vault side of Bull Moose, fork oversized pistons to life, give top volume to Scruggs solo _(Flint Hill Special)_, engineer four-wheel Wicker breakaway from the high ground on a heading east to west through the flood, skirt-ing south side of red-stone rocket, confirming almost at once the principle that under certain definable circumstances, something has to give — in this case, not antler nor tree fork nor synthetic line capable of resisting 2000-plus pounds of stress but old jungle hammock, weary, perhaps, of so much hanging around, torn in two with a rattling bang, half left fastened to the sacred grove, half flying between legs of Old Moose charging.

Elapsed time from point of departure to point of arrival: 26 seconds. Engine off. Scruggs silenced mid-tune as if by the bow of a fiddle.

"Ma'am! Ah don't take it kandly yew startin' without me! Yew hair!"

Measuring from canyon floor 260 feet up Cholla Rock, the first 60 feet angled at 45 degrees, the next 200 at 70 degrees; and at exactly that point, just there precisely, a nicely booted foot moving up from the fourth to the third web step of a four-step *étrier* hung from *piton* recently driven into crack. And from approximately five feet above that raised foot, give or take an inch or so, a pretty voice coming all that distance down in reply to one of Lubbock's favorite sons:

"Drop dead! Will you!"

Hour one. Jay-D Wicker, Sierra jacket size of beanbag now in pocket of climbing pack (with two 150-foot coils of Perlon rope, one one-quarter-inch, one three-eighths-inch, and other miscellanies); black form-fit T-shirt snug over lats, pecs, traps, delts; 16-inch arms abulge from truly herculean effort to gain elevation at faster rate than enemy; bush hat knocked back on first difficult move, held by chin strap; two bandoleers, shoulder to hip, shoulder to hip, each festooned with nuts and wedges, *pitons* and carabiners, *étriers*, lap links, cliff-hangers, crack tacks, bongs, brake bars, daisy chains, copperheads; quick-draw hammer holster low on hip; belt-worn bolt kit, dolt bolt hangers, studs, drills.... All standing easily now — although huffing and puffing a little — edge of right Galibier rock shoe on one-eighth-inch flake, 260 feet above the flood, west face, Cholla Rock (hot sun, blue sky, swallows swooping); left hand clipping carabiner into eye of *piton* driven and left by another party earlier that morning (said party hard-hatted and hard at it 360 feet high on same west face, feet wedged in long vertical crack, waist secured to length of web sling looped around chock stone, hands above head, about to drive four-inch bong into same crack above chock stone. Short pants. Long legs.).

"Ma'am!"

"What is it?!"

"Yew left a *pyton* down year!"

Early, tentative blows on bong. Hammer on high (thock-thock).

"Hair!"

"*Please* feel free to use it!"

"Ah intend to!"

Pretty face looking down with, well, a certain disapproval. "I am sure you need *all* the help you can get!"

"Not tall!"

"Someone else! Almost anyone else I can think of! Would have selected his own route! Would have used his imagination! Would have shown a *modicum* of pride! Would *not* have turned a potentially beautiful climb into an absurd race!"

"Well, how come *yew* snuck up year 'fore sunup?"

Rain of blows on bong (thock-thock, thick-thack, bang-bong-bang). Hostility redirected. Metal to stone. Desert falcons glide from aeries on high to see going out and down small chips once part of wall.

"AND DON'T DROP ROCKS ON MAH HAID!"

"I am," she said, "*exceedingly* sorry."

Hours two and three. Enemy climbing carefully but well ascends 100 additional feet up long vertical crack, exits finally at start of two-inch ledge extruded horizontally across west face. Enemy traverses this ledge north to south until reaches start of natural chimney. Pauses to glance over shoulder at point high on vertical crack where:

Jay-D Wicker, formerly of Lubbock, Texas, but recently on the road, heroically toils to make up for lost time. Makes it to small but tricky overhanging section of wall, 430 vertical feet above driver's seat of Old Bull Moose, a like distance below final objective (the summit, that is), huffing and puffing, looking over what is in the vernacular of the overreachers "an interesting technical dilemma."

"Ma'am?"

"What is it?"

"Did yew use steps to mount this-year overhang?"

"I did not."

"Yew free-clammed it?"

"I did."

"Whee-oo," Jay-D said. Respectfully.

Moment of silence between these two and all other living things within earshot save the flood that burbled far below, sun bright in its riffles and rills.

"Whee-oo," Jay-D said again.

"If you will reach your left hand to the edge of the overhang. . . ." Said patiently and with kindness, as if to a small but earnest child. "And then move it slowly to the left, you will find a substantial hold."

"M-m-m – rat!"

"On the wall about sixteen inches above the toe of your right shoe and about four inches out from the crack, concealed by a nubbin lip, you will find a solution hole large enough to accommodate your toe and angled in such a way that counterforce can be applied between your left hand and *left* foot."

"M-m-m – rat!"

"This will give you the leverage necessary to circumvent the overhang."

"Ma'am?"

"Circumvent," she said, "the overhang."

"*Lord,*" Jay-D said.

"Now that I have solved that problem for you, in addition to leaving *pitons* at several critical points along the way, *plus* doing all the route finding, I am sure you will agree you are no longer handicapped by the early start I had. Do you agree?"

Jay-D, heavily engaged in circumventing the overhang, sweaty face, crimson ears, bulging neck, all orifices tightly puckered, unable to reply.

Hours four and five. Enemy leaving narrow traversing ledge enters chimney, three feet wide, 125 feet high, places back and hands against close wall, feet against far wall, and ascends by means of a clean, uncomplicated motion. Exits chimney to free-climb additional 100 feet to small sit-down ledge. Drives *piton* into crack on adjacent wall, suspends pack and hard hat from same, shakes out hair, turns, sits, back of denim shirt (sweat-soaked) to wall, legs dangling over ledge. Peers out now and then between small neat bites of cucumber sandwich and slugs of celery tonic to see:

Jay-D Wicker emerge bloodied but unbowed from bout with tiny unseen cactus in last section of chimney. Huffing, puffing, bandoleers arattle (click-click, ching-ching), head down, climbing up, inch by inch, foot by foot, angle of climb 75 degrees, difficulty of climb 5.8 on the decimal system scale, elevation above ground 585 feet, 590 feet, 610 feet, 615 feet . . . . .616 feet. . . . .617 feet . . . . .617 feet. . . . .

"Are you —" she started to say.

"HAILP!!!"

Airborne. Upside down high above Old Bull Moose, latissimus spread in imitation of eagles but of small use, due to unfavorable ratio between amount to be lifted and amount of lift; folly of *hubris* flashing before eyes ("Boy, yew got yore feet planted smack in midair!"). A graceless and apparently endless fall until — no *deus ex machina* here but simply the system at work — he was stopped WHUMP! by *piton* and ten-foot loop of quarter-inch Perlon rope. *Lord! Breath-taking!* Hung by his own petard, all adangle while something echoed unnaturally from canyon wall to canyon wall, a scream. . . . His? . . . Hers?

"Are you all right?" (Right-right-right?)

"Yas!" (Yas-yas-yas!)

"What did you do?" (Do-do-do?)

"Ah fail!" (Ail-ail-ail!)

"Well, I know that!" (At-at-at!)

"Danged flake busted on me!" (Onme-onme-onme!)

"Would you like me to lower a rope?" (Arope-arope-arope?)
"Hail, no!" (Oh-oh-oh!)
"I'm glad there wasn't a tragedy!" (Agedy-agedy-agedy!)
"So my!" (My-my-my!)

Hours six and seven. The enemy, having in light of certain unexpected and fairly substantial delays in the troop movements of the other side lingered at lunch, savored the sun (which for those who have lost sight of such things has already passed its zenith), eaten a high-protein energy bar, *rises* finally to ascend slowly but with great skill to a ledge exactly 850 feet above the ground and ten feet below the virginal apogee of Cholla Rock, Kachina Canyon, Arizona, U.S.A., where, for the first time, trouble is encountered in form of an expanse of stone angled at 80 degrees, glass-smooth except for small V-shaped crack six inches beyond tips of fingers, even when at great risk to self standing on pack on ledge, denim shirt unbuttoned to improve reach. Struggles – unkind to put it this way – *manfully* for 20 minutes to no avail, when at long last, just below ledge:

Our hero arrives. Huff-huff. Puff-puff. Wondering what is up.

"I am truly sorry to have to say this," she explains. "But I need one of your nuts."

There follows here a brief explanatory paragraph for benefit of those who have not lately climbed high-angle rock. Rest may proceed directly to subsequent section, where Jay-D Wicker says. . . .

Definition of nut (and, indirectly, of nutters and nutting): Recent technological innovation in sport of rock-climbing, scorned by purists, perhaps, but hailed by most as aesthetically acceptable breakthrough. Certain distinct advantages over more traditional *piton.* But picture first a common nut, hexagonally shaped, with, say, a three-eighths-inch-diameter hole, originally threaded but threads removed by means of small rat-tailed file. And picture, fixed to this now-smooth-sided hole, a six-inch length of three-sixteenth-inch airplane cable, looped at its lower end. *Used as follows:* Wedge nut in crack on rock face, cable loop hanging down. Clip carabiner to loop. Clip rope (or *étrier*) through carabiner (as in classic climbing technique). *Advantages:* Nuts just as strong as *pitons* but lighter. Easier to place. Easier to remove. *And,* because cable is stiff, nut can be raised to and placed in crack six or eight inches beyond climber's reach, whereas *piton* cannot. A point that will soon be brought to Jay-D Wicker's attention as he says. . . .

"Whut fer?"

"If you will raise the brim of your hat," the enemy replied, coolly over right shoulder, "you will see that I have reached a virtually impassable section of wall, *quite* devoid of cracks, nubbins, flakes and other natural aids, *except* for one small V-shaped fissure that lies six or eight inches beyond my reach."

"Ah'll take care of it, ma'am, if yew'll jest step down. . . ."

"I have no intention of 'stepping down.' "

Flourish of temper. Trumpeting of male prerogative.

"Ma'am, if yew ain't e-quipped fer this clam, be daysent and say so! Hair!"

A turning now inch by inch of booted feet on pack on ledge until enemy profiled to wall, looking down.

"What did you say?"

"Ah said, if yew ain't *e*-quipped —"

"It is not a matter of my not being equipped! I have a perfectly good bolt kit and am quite capable of fixing a bolt in no more than twelve minutes. However, I am sure you will agree that *inasmuch as* we have managed to ascend this entire rock without using a single bolt, it would be unthinkable to use one now. It would violate the aesthetic of the climb in ways too obvious to mention. A nut will be faster, will serve exactly the same purpose and, once it has served that purpose, can be removed without leaving a trace of our having passed this way." Pause. No reply from hero standing on small holds just below ledge, face level with enemy's pack, uptilted to allow view. "As for my shirt being unbuttoned," she continued, "which seems to have 'attracted your attention,' as you would say, I did that in an attempt to increase my reach. My position at this moment is too precarious to attempt a rebuttoning. I hope the redness around your ears is a result of your exertions and not of some ridiculous postpubescent projection."

"Lord hailp us," Jay-D said.

And the Lord, who had first helped others (falcons and mice among them) to this high place, did help these two, the first of their kind, who appeared finally up over the edge, hard hat first, followed closely by bush hat second. Moment of illuminating awe: long view out, 1000-foot red canyon walls, snow-rimmed juniper and jack pine, ice-blue sky, westering sun; long view down, 860 feet Old Bull Moose reduced in distance tiny toy, chrome reflecting flood-dazzle; close view summit, size of baseball infield studded with mesquite and, appropriate to image, one diamond-shaped meltwater pool.

"Isn't it wonderful!" she exclaimed. "Isn't it marvelous! Have you ever seen anything so, so, so *exquisite*!"

No reply from Jay-D Wicker, who stood like a sweat-soaked question mark not far from ultimate edge.

"What's the matter?" she asked.

"Nothin'."

"Of course there is. You look simply awful."

Silence.

"Well?" she insisted.

"Ah'm *de*-pressed."

"What on earth for? How could you possibly be depressed after as invigorating a climb as we have just had, in the presence of this grandeur?"

"Ah ain't never bin whupped by a fay-male. It don't seem rat."

"I am *not* a 'fay-male,' " she said. "I am a person. The only reason you were 'whupped', as you say, is that you, having clearly underestimated my ability, *insisted* on turning what might have been a delightful climb into a neurotic sweepstakes —"

"Ah cain't hailp it!" Jay-D blurted. "Ah let down mah sad!"

"Oh, really," she said. "For heaven's sake. The idea that men and women make up opposing sides in some kind of sexual war is not only absurd but also, in light of recent years, anachronistic. Furthermore, there is absolutely *no* justification for raising the climb we have just completed to the level of a metaphor."

Silence then, save the distant and brief scurry of one small unfortunate rodent and a beating of falcon wings.

"Oh, dear," she said.

"Whut?"

"It's just that . . . well . . . life is *so* ephemeral."

Removed hard hat. Shook long hair down. Looked at him. Smiled.

"What's your name?"

"Jay-D Wacker."

"My name is Amanda Barrymore-Fitzgerald. I am a senior at Wheaton College, which is a rather good women's school located in Norton, Massachusetts."

Extended her hand. Briefly, he took it. It was hot. She opened a pack pocket then and got out some soap, not onion but lemon-scented.

"I'm a perfect mess," she said. "You are, too. Shall we 'bite the apple,' as they say?"

"Ma'am?"

"Bathe," she said. "Before descending."

Large mesquite bush atop 860-foot rock pinnacle deep in canyon, northeastern Arizona. From low branch on close side of bush (our point of view), a familiar flag flying in what has become a warm, satisfying breeze. In diamond-shaped melt-water pool nearby, a being too voluptuous to have sprung from a rib sits, the water rising to point just below her newly soaped navel. She is waiting for a man to join her, a man whom she has only recently met but for whom – and for reasons she really could not have articulated – she has developed a certain fondness. He appears at last, a well-muscled youth, blue eyes, blond hair, altogther naked except for an old bush hat which he holds by the brim to cover, well, his old bush.

"I don't believe it!" she cries. "Not you! Not the Old Bull Moose of the Woods!"

"Ma'am –"

"Oh, this is priceless!"

"Ma'am, fact is –"

"And they say *we* need liberating!"

He shrugs, letting go the hat brim to gesture helplessly. The hat, in defiance of certain of Newton's laws, not falling to the ground but staying in place as if on rack.

"Fact is, ma'am, Ah'm aroused!"

Bright but not unkind laughter from pool fills the rare air there like clatter of coins – no – like stained glass breaking – no – like antic tropical bird. . . .

"Come here," she says. "You silly boy."

Time passes. It is an interim of exploration, of discovery, of gentleness and liberation; and it is, in spite of experiments to the contrary, a close and private thing that can no more pass through the point of a pen than can a butterfly's wing. In the interest of objectivity and truth, however, we will set down the single line of dialog spoken during the passage of this time (and spoken near the end, and with reverence):

"*Lord,* ma'am. Did yew learn this at Waitin College?"

And here at last an anticlimax, a denouement, a tying up

of loose ends wrapped in end-of-story rhetoric suitable to the epic structure of the piece (and setting, too, symbolic). A glimpse of the morning after.

Old Noah-Body, Indian chief, alert in coffin by aspen gate, observes through wintry eyes and early April mist one antlered ark advancing on the surface of the flood, complete now with one of this and one of that (Earl Scruggs and Lester Flatt), the Old Bull Moose returning. High ground at last (with help of Lord's wind) and passing under elevated aspen gate in cloud of dust and final Horny-ho-ho. Jay-D Wicker at the walnut wheel and – riding shotgun, shall we say? – the heroine of the tale, tresses secured under borrowed bush hat, Amanda Barrymore-Fitzgerald, to be known affectionately for some time to come as his 'swate thang,' all fading now, music, motion and immutability, not into the west but toward the east, where the sun has risen and spreads its supernal glow across the continent in benign benediction to all created things.

Goodbye, my friends. God bless.

From 1968 through 1976 I taught a fiction writing seminar at Northeastern University in Boston. On my way to and from the classes, I often found myself walking by the Prudential Tower, with its unique facade; and the more I walked by it, the more I became sure it could be climbed.

One day, just to get the feel of it, I climbed a little way up the facade and drew the attention of a security guard. He asked me what I was doing, and I replied I was doing some research for a short story I hoped to write. He took me up to the office of the man who was chief of security for the Prudential complex. This man's office was very high up in the tower, and he sat at his desk, with his back to the glass wall that gave his visitor a spectacular view out over the city of Boston.

I asked him if he would tell me about the security system in the Prudential Tower. He did so with a great deal of pride. The building was, as far as he was concerned, completely secure. I said, Well suppose somebody wanted to break into your office here, after the building was closed for the night? They couldn't do that, he said. What if they came in through that window behind your desk? I said. He looked amazed. We're forty-two stories above the ground, he said. There's no way anybody is going to come through that window. I said I thought a climber could, and that I was going to write a story about that. He looked at me as if he thought I was a pretty funny fellow—which I guess sometimes I am.

I think this story appeared before George Willig made his classic ascent of the World Trade Center. If so, I get a kick out of thinking that Willig's climb might have been a case of life imitating art.

Written: Bow Lake, Strafford, New Hampshire; Autumn, 1974
First Published: *Playboy,* August, 1975

B-TOWER WEST WALL

Let me confess this to you. They killed Baker as soon as we went in the door. They shot him twice in the chest: two men in business suits; pistols with silencers. Baker was a big man, but the bullets stopped him as if he had walked into a tree. I think he was dead before he hit the floor, but he lay there for a while with his legs thrashing and my son Chip, who had always thought a lot of Baker, pressed his small face against the front of my parka so he wouldn't have to watch.

"Dad, Dad," he pleaded, as if he wanted me to explain what was happening, to make it not true. I couldn't. All I could do was hold him and die with him, if that's what it was going to be. He was 12, and except for the television news, where it never seems quite real, he had not seen a man get killed before. I had, but never like this.

It was a few minutes after nine p.m. We had spent the weekend in New Hampshire, climbing rock in Huntington Ravine, had just got back to the city. Baker had parked his truck under the building, had come up for a drink. I was a widower, he was divorced. We had served together, Special Forces, Vietnam, back when it had begun. Now he was dead. I looked away.

All the drapes in the apartment were drawn, though I remembered having left them open. Most of the lights were on. I could hear the traffic on Tremont Street, six stories down: sirens and horns.

"Shut the door, McKim," one of the two men said to the other. They both wore gloves. This one was young, late 20s, medium build. His hair was red and longish and crossed his forehead in bangs. He had wash-blue eyes and a lopsided nose and when he spoke, the tone of his voice was persuasively calm, as if in his view Baker's dying counted for nothing at all.

"Look," I said, trying to keep my voice steady. "I don't know what this is. I don't care what you do to me. But let my boy go."

"There's some clothes in the bedroom," the redhead said. "Sports jackets, slacks, street shoes. Put them on, both you and the kid. There's an empty overnight bag in the closet. You put your climbing shit in that bag: pants, boots, parka. The kid won't need his. McKim will go in there with you while you change."

I nodded. McKim came up next to me. He was a couple of years older than the redhead, dark complected, heavier set. He had the thick neck and wrists of a man who might have been a wrestler once or a catcher in a trapeze act. His suit was expensive, $250, maybe $300. It smelled like cloves.

"You screw off or make noise or give McKim any trouble," the redhead went on, "and your kid will wind up as dead as your buddy. You got that?"

I told him I did.

McKim went with us into my bedroom, where we changed clothes the way we'd been told to. My wife's picture was on the dresser. When she had turned 30, she started having headaches but was misdiagnosed. By the time the doctors got it right, she was a long way toward being dead.

McKim took off his gloves and inspected his nails. They were cut short and filed smooth. He had not closed the bedroom door. I could hear the redhead talking on the living-room phone. "Yeah, yeah, we've got them," I heard him say. "Tell Sights to meet us there in half an hour. Yeah, yeah. No sweat."

Chip looked up at me. He was in his jacket and slacks now and looked nice, the way he always did whenever I took him out to a good restaurant, except he was pale and his lip was shaking; but he was holding on and I was proud of him for that and scared.

"We'll be OK," I told him. "We'll do what they want us to do and when they're through with us, they'll let us go." I glanced at McKim, hoping he'd back me up on that.

He didn't.

We took the elevator to the garage. They had a limousine waiting, a dark-blue late-model Caddy with a phone antenna in the center of its trunk. An old man drove. He wore plaid slacks and a white shirt with the sleeves rolled back and he didn't ask anybody where he should go and nobody told him. The redhead sat in front. Chip and I sat in back, along with McKim and my overnight bag. I held Chip's hand. It was early September, cool enough so that the old man had the heater on low. There was an east wind coming in off the harbor; the few women on the street who wore skirts had to hold them down with their hands. We drove west on Commonwealth.

"Dad," Chip whispered after a while. "Where are they taking us?"

"I don't know," I said. "To the Carlyle, maybe." That's a new 30-story hotel in the Back Bay. We pulled into the half-circle drive at the main entrance. The redhead turned around and looked at me.

"I'll be behind the kid when we go in," he said in the calm way he had of saying things. "You won't try any shit."

"No," I said.

Once the four of us were out, the old man drove the Caddy away.

The lobby of the Carlyle was jammed: a pharmacists' convention going on; men with short haircuts and plastic I.D.s pinned to medium-wide lapels. No cops in sight. I wouldn't have called them if there had been. McKim went to the main desk and got a room key, then we took a crowded elevator to the fourth floor, which I knew was the first floor of rooms.

"He's already here," McKim said as we walked down a long corridor. The carpet was deep blue and smelled as if one of the conventioneers had tossed his cookies onto it.

"I told him half an hour," the redhead said.

"Yeah, well, he's here now. He took the other key. I don't like that shit."

"He's all right."

"He sucks," McKim said.

"He does his job; forget it. Open the door."

We had reached the end of the corridor. McKim let us in to room number 418. Once we were in, he pulled the door shut behind him. The room was smoky, the drapes drawn. A wispy, thin kid in black slacks and a blue button-down sat sprawled on one of two queen-size beds. He was smoking a cigarette, watching TV highlights of a pro game that had been played earlier that afternoon: Patriots-Bills. Baker and I had bet on it driving back from Huntington Ravine. Baker had won. I had told him to come on up for a drink.

The kid had dark hair with a bald spot the size of a butter plate. He wore the kind of heavy-framed glasses people used to like in the Fifties. The lenses were the thickest I'd ever seen. They magnified his pupils so that when he looked at you it was as if he were seeing you through a couple of stewed prunes.

"Is this the man?" he said without getting up.

"Yeah, right," the redhead said.

"He looks older than I thought he would. Why did you bring the boy?"

"Never mind the boy, Sights. You just get your shit together. Show him what he's going to do."

Sights stood up, stretched, yawned. He may have been tired, but I'd have bet right then he was nervous, too. Chip's hand was small and moist in mine. I loved him. I've heard about fathers who don't love their kids, but I've never met one. I guess I've been lucky.

"You've done a considerable amount of direct-aid climbing, is that correct?" Sights said.

"I've done some," I said. He sounded like a third-string professor at the kind of college I might have made if I'd had time to make one.

"Long's Peak Diamond, El Capitan, The Fisher Towers. . . ."
He ticked them off.

"They're standard climbs," I told him. "I haven't done anything a lot of other people haven't done just as good or better."

"You were profiled in the *Globe*."

"Once. Five years ago. I haven't been west of Chicago since."

"But you still climb, correct?"

"I do when I can. Look, I'd like to know what this is all
about."

"Tell him," McKim said. There was an ice bucket and bottle of Chivas on the vanity. McKim was pouring himself a
drink. The redhead had gone into the can.

"They want you to do a climb for them," Sights explained.
"What climb?"

He went to the window and opened the drapes. The room
we were in had a close view of the Bennington Tower, a floodlit
52-story high-rise.

"That one," Sights said. "They need to get into an office on
the forty-second floor."

The hotel was part of the Bennington Plaza complex, the
biggest and newest collection of buildings in Boston. The Bennington Tower was the hub of the plaza wheel. It had over
1,000,000 square feet of office space and a restaurant on top
where Chip and I had gone a lot. He liked the view and a
waitress named Sadie who would always tell him Chip was
hip and bring him desserts that weren't on the menu.

"Right now we are less than a hundred feet above the plaza
roof," Sights said. He'd gotten a green Forrest pack from the
closet and taken from it what looked like photocopies of building blueprints and a half-dozen original diagrams. He'd spread
them out on the bed near the door. McKim sat on one side of
him, I sat on the other. Chip and the redhead sat in the chairs.
"The facade lights go off at midnight. That's because of the energy crisis. They used to stay on all night." He blinked at McKim

through his thick glasses, as if he was proud of having that kind of information.

"So what do we do?" McKim wanted to know. "Just cut the shit."

"As soon as the facade lights are off, you rappel from here down to the plaza roof. He'll show you how; it's not difficult. Then you walk three hundred feet across the plaza roof to the corner of the west wall of the Tower. That's the one we're looking at."

"Which corner?" McKim said.

"The left one as you face it. There's less traffic on that side, less reflected light. The facade itself consists of hard aluminum mullions that run symmetrically in rows up the wall, and hard aluminum sills that run symmetrically across it. Where they intersect, they form rectangular boxes. Each box is two and a half feet wide and six and a half feet high. There are over six thousand of these boxes on each of the four walls. They are functional where they frame a window, decorative where they do not, but they are all made of the same material. The mullions and sills are three inches thick and extend seven inches out from the building itself."

Sights showed us how it looked. His blueprints and diagrams were clear, sharp and detailed; they showed the various elevations of the Tower, the curtain-wall design, the corridors, stair wells, elevators.

"Why the corner?" I asked.

"Because it's the only place where the sills are not flush with the wall. You've got a two-inch gap where you can loop a sling and hang a stirrup."

"What happens when we get to the forty-second floor?"

"The office they want is in the center of the wall. You will have to traverse ninety feet, stepping from box to box."

"Any protection on that?"

"Nothing I could figure," Sights admitted. "But with seven-inch platforms to stand on, I don't see why you should have any trouble."

I studied the drawings he'd made, tried to memorize them, tried to discover a way out for Chip and me.

"All right," I said finally. "Suppose we don't have any trouble. We're forty-two stories up and I'm ninety feet out on the wall. I've got nothing to anchor to and no way to protect him coming across —"

"That was the most difficult problem I had," Sights admitted. He looked satisfied as hell. He got up and went to the closet, came back with what looked like a two-and-a-half-foot length of one-inch pipe with a chrome sleeve and rubber cups at each end.

"Have you ever seen one of these?" he asked. I told him I hadn't. McKim told him he had.

"It's a portable chinning bar," Sights explained. "It's designed for doors. You turn the sleeve and the ends tighten against the frame. If you use enough torque, a man weighing three hundred pounds could hang from it all day."

"So what?" McKim said. "What good is that going to do him?"

"I put that in the box in front of the window you want," I said.

"Correct," Sights said. "That will give McKim a fixed rope on the traverse and something to tie on to while he works on the window."

"Very beautiful," the redhead said. I didn't know he'd been listening, but I guess he had, and Sights looked pleased.

"How the fuck do we get down?" McKim wanted to know.

"You traverse back to the corner and make four rappels. Then you walk back across the roof of the plaza. You will have a penlight to signal with. When you do, Red will lower a rope and up you come."

"Have you got ascenders?" I asked.

"Jumars," he said. "Two pair in the pack. Carabiners, five-step web stirrups, slings, everything you need. There are three hundred-and-fifty-foot ropes in the closet: two for you to take and one to leave here."

"It sounds like a hell of a lot of trouble," I said. "Why not take the elevator and jimmy the office door?"

"The offices shut down at five p.m.," he told me. "Seven days a week. The elevators are computer programmed. Once the cleaning crews are out — usually by eleven — the only one that operates is the express to the restaurant. All the office doors have electromagnetic locks. There are infrared scanners in the halls and emergency stair wells. Pinkertons patrol the lobby and the plaza outside the building."

"How thick is the window?" McKim wanted to know.

"They vary, depending on wind load and building height. That high, you should figure half-inch glass in a double-glazed unit."

"What about alarms?"

"There aren't any. Except for the floodlights and the Pinkertons in the plaza, there is no outside security at all."

"How come?"

"They think it's impossible for anyone to go up that way."

"How the fuck do you know what they think?" McKim said.

Sights smiled.

"I asked their security chief," he said. "I told him I was doing a term paper."

I asked McKim if he'd ever climbed before, though I knew he hadn't. He shook his head.

"How high will we be?" I said.

Sights blinked. "The Tower is eight hundred feet. By the time you get to the forty-second floor, you will be about 600 feet above the plaza roof."

"That's a long way up for anybody who hasn't climbed," I said. "If I'm going to do it, I'd rather do it alone."

"You don't pick locks, do you?" the redhead put in. He had got up and was pouring himself a drink. He wasn't really asking, but I told him I didn't pick locks. "Don't worry about McKim," he said. "You just get him to the right window and he'll take care of the rest of it."

They paid Sights off and he left. I couldn't tell how much they gave him, but it was in cash and it looked like a lot.

"Are you going to do it, Dad?" Chip asked me. He'd got up to give me his chair and I'd taken it and pulled him down onto my lap. We'd scrubbed up at noon in a mountain stream in New Hampshire. His hair smelled terrific: like sun and leaves.

"Sure," I said, trying to sound calm. "It should be easier than what we were doing in Huntington."

"Will it take a long time?"

"I don't think so. Couple of hours, maybe."

"What should I do?"

"Sit tight."

"Do I have to do what he says?"

"Yes."

"Can't I —"

"You do what he says. I don't want you to worry about me; I'll be fine. OK?"

"Sure. OK."

I held him tight. Ever since they'd shot Baker, I'd been try- ing to figure a way out of this jam we were in, but so far noth- ing had come up right, everything too risky, too liable to get us both killed. All I could do was wait and hope. McKim had gone into the can to change clothes. When he came out, he was wearing fatigue pants, a black sweat shirt like mine and a pair of Royal Robbins Klettershuhs. He had a holster sus- pended from a wide black leather loop on his left shoulder. The holster had been especially made for a modified automatic with a silencer. He stood next to one of the beds, shoving his wallet, keys and change into his trouser pockets. I looked at him. I'd been right about his build. He looked strong as hell.

"What time is it?" he asked.

"Ten-thirty," the redhead said. "You've got an hour and a half."

The facade lights went off at 12 and we were on the pla- za roof at 12:10. McKim had taken the bottom half of the window unit out; I'd used the vanity to anchor our rappel. Once we were down, he blinked his penlight and Red hauled up the rope. When I thought about Chip alone in that room with one of the men who had killed Baker, I felt weak, as if someone had drained off half my blood.

It was dark and cold and I could feel the wind coming at me damp and salty as we hurried across the plaza roof. The roof surface was fixed gravel and what noise we made going across was lost in the noise of the late traffic on the city streets. The stream of headlights, the glitter and flare of restaurant signs, movie marquees and arc lamps all seemed a million miles away to me, like a promised land I'd only be able to dream about and never reach. Where I was was dark and cold and deadly with McKim just beside me, sure of himself because he knew I wouldn't do anything to risk my son's life.

"Get started," he told me when we got to the northwest corner of the Tower. I wondered how sure of himself he really was about this climb we were about to try. And I wondered, too, what they were after in that office on the 42nd floor. Something big. Something worth killing an innocent man for.

I uncoiled one of the ropes we had, tied one end around McKim's solid waist, the other around my own. He would carry the second coiled rope and the Forrest pack, in which he'd put his tools. I showed him how he should follow me after I'd gone up one lead.

"Get started," he said. And I did.

I went up a rope's length, moving as quickly as I could. Sights had been right. The aluminum sills curved at the corner and gapped from the wall. I'd stand on one, reach half a foot over my head, loop a sling, hang a five-step web stirrup. Then I'd go up the stirrup, gripping the adjacent vertical mullions to steady myself. Once I was standing on the next higher sill, I'd reach down, retrieve the stirrup and repeat the process. It was awkward at first, but I got on to it quickly.

I ran the rope out, anchored myself and gave McKim a

snug belay as he came up with his own stirrup and sling. I found it was easiest to stand sideways on the sill with my back to the wind that was blowing hard along the north wall of the Tower. I was already higher than we'd been in the hotel. I could see the lighted window of 418, but Red had drawn the drapes again and I couldn't see in. God help Chip, I thought, if anything goes wrong.

McKim came up. I could hear him grunting and cursing just below me in the dark. There were no stars visible, no moon. The light from the streets below bounced off a lowering overcast of cloud. Though they were just 300 feet away, I had trouble seeing the corners of the hotel, could not see the upper floors at all. If anyone on the street happened to glance up at the Bennington Tower, there was no chance he was going to see us, and just now I was glad of that.

"Far enough," I told McKim. "Tie yourself in. I'm going up."

We made the 42nd floor in five leads. McKim got slower on each one. During the fourth and fifth leads, he lost his grip on the mullions twice and fell back and I had to stop him with the rope. He was winded, silent and, I think, more scared than he'd figured on being. At the end of it, we were 600 feet above the plaza roof, shrouded in fog. The mullions and sills were cold and wet. The big panes of glass on the north wall creaked and popped in the wind.

"*Christ*," McKim croaked. He stood just below me. I could hear him, but I couldn't see him.

"Tie yourself in," I said. "Give me the extra rope and the chinning bar." When he did, I tied the chinning bar to the back of my waist loop, then made one end of the extra rope fast to the sill just above my head, draping the loose coils over my left shoulder. I told McKim how he should do the traverse. I took the penlight from him and told him I'd signal when I wanted him to start. He sounded as if he wanted to talk some more, but I didn't and I stepped very slowly and carefully from the corner into the first box on the west wall.

It was bad standing there: too close, too tight. I felt as if someone had put me in a coffin. I wanted to step back to get some breathing room, but all I had to stand on was that seven-inch sill. I kept my left arm high so the coils of the extra rope wouldn't spill off and I moved from the first box to the second. I had to squeegee water off the surface of the mullions before I could get a fair grip on them. My leather belaying gloves were soaked.

According to Sights's diagram, the window of the office they wanted was 30 boxes in from the corner of the 42nd floor. I counted each one as I stepped around, then rested a few seconds, then stepped around to the next. The weight of the chinning bar and the extra rope pulled like a hand behind me. Twice I pressed my face against the cold window glass and rested a full minute. My heart tripped in my chest. Sooner or later, I knew I'd have to make a move, for Chip's sake and my own, but I still couldn't think what it would be. The redhead and McKim weren't going to let us go, I was pretty sure of that. We'd seen them kill Baker and they hadn't told Sights anything about it nor explained to him why they'd brought Chip along. My guess was they'd be needing Sights again and that's why they were keeping his nose clean. I guessed they wouldn't be needing us again.

As I kept moving toward the center of the west wall, I heard sirens in South Boston, a long way off, and jets taking off and coming in at Logan, in spite of the fog. I wished Chip and I were on one of them, going to Puerto Rico, maybe, someplace in the sun.

When I was able to, I set the chinning bar high up between the mullions that framed the window they wanted. I couldn't see anything inside. I screwed the bar in as tightly as I could, yanked it a couple of times, then slowly let it take my weight until I was hanging from it. I weighed 190 and it held me solidly. I pulled all the slack out of the extra rope, tied it to the bar, stepped one box over and signaled for McKim to come ahead.

Somehow he managed to spot that wink of light through the fog; I think he would have spotted it if I'd been three states away. He came quickly, wanting to get it over with, feeling safer with the fixed rope to clip to than I'd felt without it.

"Tie onto the bar," I told him when he reached it. "It's safe. You can hang from it, lean back, whatever you want."

He didn't answer, which was just as well, because at that moment I saw what I was going to do, all laid out like a color film on a small white screen in my brain.

McKim cut out the lower half of the outside panel of glass and taped it to the upper half. Then he cut out the lower half of the inside panel and dropped it onto the carpeted floor of the office. He did it fast and clean and told me to follow him in.

It was pitch-black inside and smelled of cleaning fluids. I could hear a soft whirring sound, as if the blower in a heating unit had come on. According to Sights's diagram of the suite, there were three rooms: the private office we were in, a larger reception area, and a file room. McKim got a three-battery flash out of the pack and told me to follow him. We were still roped up. I coiled the slack as we went. He headed for the file room. Shadows cast by the beam of his light bobbed and shrank.

The files were color-coded and numbered. From what I could see, there were a lot of them: They covered three walls of the room from floor to ceiling. McKim moved the flash impatiently; it appeared that he knew exactly what he was looking for but couldn't find it. The cabinets were heavy-gauge steel and locked. The colors were pastel: yellow, orange, buff, green, blue. The numbers seemed to run in series: A/100, A/110, and so on. McKim swore. He was on his hands and knees now, moving slowing, checking the numbers on the bottom row.

"OK, I got it," he said finally. "Hold the fucking light."

I put the beam on the green vinyl pack. He got out an aerosol can of silicone and a small leather packet of lock picks, which he unrolled on the carpeted floor. He blew a jet of sili-

cone into the file lock, chose one of the picks and went to work.
I couldn't see my watch, but I don't think it took him a minute
and a half to open the drawer. It was blue and the number on
it was N/100. It rolled out quietly. McKim reached in. I could
see his thick wrists and stubby fingers moving over the legal-
size folders, quickly at first, then slowing as he neared the
back.

"OK, got it," he said, this time more to himself than to me.
He pulled out what looked like a pocket-size ledger, and then
two more.

"Give me some light," he said. I did. He sat on the carpet,
looking at the ledgers. Each of them was bound in worn red
leather with a gold Roman numeral embossed on the center
of the front cover: I, II, III. The ledger sheets themselves were
coded and filled with neat columns of figures. McKim grinned.
I hadn't seen him do that before. I stood over him, the coils
of rope in my left hand, the flash in my right. It was quiet in
the room, as if the walls and floor and ceiling were all six feet
thick, as if we were inside the main vault of a bank.

"Fucking Nancarrow," he said, looking up at me.

I nodded as though I didn't know what he was talking
about, but I did and he knew I did.

"If you've got what we came for, let's get out of here," I told
him.

"We just blew that son of a bitch away," he replied.

"OK, swell," I said. "My boy's waiting for me. I'd like to get
back to him."

"Fuck you," McKim said. He started to get up. He was about
halfway up when I kicked him. I kept the light on the left side
of his face and kicked him just under the chin, the way I would
have punted a football. I heard his teeth snap, heard him grunt,
saw him bang against the file cabinets, then sag to his knees.
I was edgy as hell but mad, too. I came up next to him and
swung the flash against the back of his neck. The light winked
out. I heard him groan as he went down. In the pitch-darkness

of the room, I found him, groped for the pistol in his shoulder holster. I thought he had to be damn near out, but suddenly he was boiling up under me, shoving his fist in my gut, locking his hands on my throat. I could hear him snarl, spit blood. I tried to pull his hands away but couldn't. When I began to black out, I found his pistol, with some difficulty pulled it out of the long holster, put the silencer against his heart, pulled the trigger once. It was a Beretta .380. It bucked a little. There was hardly any noise. I felt McKim slide away from me.

I could have picked up one of the office phones then and called the police. I could have told them about Baker and McKim and Sights and Nancarrow and the old man in the parking garage at my place who had probably fingered Baker while we were on our way up. I could have told them where the redhead was and how he was holding Chip as a hostage, could have let them be responsible for trying to get my son out safe, and maybe I should have, but I didn't.

I figured the way things had been going in this country for the past ten years, I'd most likely be the one they'd lock up and the redhead would go free or do short time and Chip would get killed or hurt bad when the cops raided the room. He was all I had, and if anything was going to happen to him, it was going to be my fault and not someone else's.

I found the penlight and untied the rope that still connected me to McKim. I went through his pockets. He was carrying the hotel-room key, a small bottle of glycerin, a thick roll of aluminum-backed tape, the straight-stemmed cutter he'd used on the glass, his wallet and the packet of lock picks. I took everything except the wallet. I put the ledgers in the breast zipper pocket of my parka. I put on the shoulder holster with the pistol in place.

There were a toilet and a closet in the private office where we'd come in. There were some clothes in the closet, including a couple of sports jackets. I took one and tied it around my waist. It was 1:40 a.m. From here on, I knew I was going to have to move fast and be lucky. My heart was beating as if it were coming through my shirt. The office had got cold; I was having trouble catching my breath.

I backed out of the hole McKim had made in the window, reached up for the chinning bar, pulled myself up. I couldn't see anything and because I couldn't, I felt disoriented and I closed my eyes and thought about the Bennington Tower and how Sights had said there were over 6000 boxes on any given wall and how I was now in one on the west wall, 42 floors up, standing on a seven-inch sill that helped form one of those boxes. I thought how I was exactly thirty boxes from the northwest corner and how I had made the traverse safely once without protection and how, if I was careful, I could make it again.

I untied the fixed rope at this end, let it go. I loosened the chinning bar and tied it to my belt. Then I was stepping slowly from box to box again, counting each one as I went. The mullions were cold and slippery; it was all I could do to hang on to them. My hands and forearms ached. I'd stand face in, with my soles flat and heels hanging over the 600 feet of space between me and the plaza roof. Then I'd move around the vertical mullion that separated me from the next box. When I got to the corner, the wind was blowing hard. I could hear the north wall creak and pop as if it were about to let go. I knew skyscrapers swayed with the wind and wondered how much this one was swaying right now.

I put my hand behind the gap in the corner sill and leaned back. The fixed rope lashed at my left. I squinted up. The atmosphere was heavy with the brackish smell of the harbor. A hundred and fifty feet above me, I thought I could see where the restaurant lights brightened the overcast. I checked my watch. The place was due to close in five minutes. I prayed some people had just come in or were taking their time with a late snack, as I knew they often did.

I was going up there. I was going up past the restaurant, up the building cap to the roof. There I was going to find a 100-foot antenna and a maintenance door that led to a storage room off the kitchen. The blueprints Sights had gotten had laid it all out for me, had told me everything except whether or not I could reach the roof edge from the last of the corner sills and, if I could, whether or not the door on the roof would be unlocked.

Using the stirrup, I began to move up. It seemed to take forever. I had to tell myself over and over to take it easy and not make a stupid mistake that would get me killed and probably Chip also. The wind wanted to blow the stirrup away. I could hear it crack like a flag under me when I was standing in the higher steps. My eyes streamed tears. My gloves were soaked and stiff and my fingers were numb. There were no more planes. When I listened for street noises, all I could hear was the racket the curtain wall of the building was making, the same splitting and popping noises the frozen surface of a lake will make in the dead of winter.

Come on, move, I told myself. But I was lead-footed and slow. When I finally got level with the restaurant, I gambled that no one would be looking out because of the fog and mist that wrapped the building like a bandage, and I leaned around one of the mullions and looked in.

The lights were soft. Most, but not all, of the tables were empty. I saw Sadie rolling the beef cart back toward the kitchen. I'd always liked her. She had the same kind of figure my wife had had: lean, small-breasted, graceful. If she hadn't been 15 years younger than I was, I'd have asked her out. Faintly through the double sash I could hear the music they always piped in after the gal at the piano bar quit. I wanted to be in there. I wanted to be one of the people I saw, sitting at a table, eating, drinking. When I thought about it, I felt tired, as if I couldn't go on; and sad as hell, too. I don't know why, but that's the way I felt looking into that place.

I used the penlight to check my watch. It was 2:25.

I continued climbing up the corner until I reached the roof cap. It felt like smooth wet marble under my gloved hand. The sills and mullions ended here. I held on to the last of them. Fifty feet above my head, one of the antenna lights blinked off and on at two-second intervals, giving the overcast a slight red glow. The wind rushing past the north wall tugged at my parka sleeve and pants leg.

I untied the chinning bar from my belt, screwed it out as far as it would go and shoved it up through the gap in the last sill, then tied it off with the same sling I hung the stirrup from. Then I began to go up, using the chinning bar to steady myself the same way I had used the vertical mullions before they'd run out. I balanced up on the balls of my feet, one step at a time. The stirrup wobbled under me. The wind wanted to push me back. I kept my face in the lee of the west wall, my cheek pressed against the roof cap. The chinning bar extended waist high beyond the last sill and I hung on to it and hoped to God it wasn't going to pop out on me or slip back through the gap.

According to Sights's blueprints, the roof was recessed to drain toward its center. A masonry lip four inches high and four inches thick kept any build-up of rain water from spilling over. When I finally stood gingerly on the last sill, I let go of the bar and reached up arm's length and felt with my finger tips the edge of the masonry lip. I didn't want to commit myself but knew if I was going to, I'd have to do it quickly.

I stepped up on my toes, stretched and reached until I had the lip with both hands, and I began to pull myself up. I kicked the wall with my feet, felt my forearms knot up and cramp, felt the strength begin to go out of them, knew in an instant I'd never make it. I pulled with everything I had left, wondered if the masonry was strong enough or whether it would suddenly break off in my hands and I would fall back and down all the way to the plaza roof. I cursed myself for not having rigged up some kind of protection. I closed my eyes and pulled and kicked, and just before I would have given it up, I found the chinning bar with my right foot, pushed down on it, pulled myself up and over.

For a few seconds, as I lay on the roof trying to get my wind, I had the same good feeling I'd always had whenever I'd worked hard to get to the top of something. Then, in the red glow from the antenna lights, I hurried across the roof to the raised steel hood where the maintenance door was set and I tried the door and it was locked.

Everything came down on me then, everything that had happened since McKim and his friend had killed Baker and taken Chip and me away. I wanted to scream. I wanted to smash something flat. I wanted to find the jerk-off who'd put a lock in a door like this and tie a knot in his nuts. When I tried to pick the lock with one of McKim's tools, my hands shook so badly I dropped the tool, and then all I could see was a lot of bright red with the image I had of those two pistols with silencers and Baker falling back and I took the handle of the door in both hands and began to turn it and kept turning until I heard something give and then the door was open.

A short flight of steel steps led to the storage closet. I used the penlight and went down. I could hear people talking in the kitchen. I got out of my parka and into the sports jacket I'd brought. I wouldn't look any too good, but neither did a lot of folks these days. I transferred the ledgers from the parka to my combat trousers. Then I went to the closet door, which was not locked, and I opened it a crack.

I could smell frying grease and some kind of cleanser. It was hot. Three men in white aprons and hats stood along a stainless-steel counter. They weren't looking my way. I stepped into the kitchen and was almost to the restaurant door before one of them called to me.

"Hey, no customers back here," he said.

"Sorry," I told him. "I took the wrong door. I wanted the head."

He told me where it was, but I already knew. I checked to be sure Sadie wasn't anywhere close by and then walked through the restaurant. At one of the tables I passed, a college kid in Levis and a turtleneck sweater was finishing a beef sandwich and a bottle of Bass Ale. Come as you are. That's how it was these days. For once, I was glad.

The maître de smiled at me when I walked by his station, but he was busy sorting receipts and didn't recognize me. There were a half-dozen people waiting in the lobby for the high-speed elevator. I waited with them, wondering what they'd say if they knew there was a dead man in an office on the 42nd floor and I was the one who had killed him, or what they'd say if they knew how I'd gotten in here and where I was going now and what I intended to do when I got there. Then I tried not to think about it or about anything else.

The elevator arrived at last. Nobody got off. The seven of us got on. We faced front. It took 30 seconds to go from the 52nd floor to the main lobby.

The place was crawling with Pinkertons. I stayed with the group until I was in that section of the plaza that joined the Bennington Tower with the Carlyle Hotel. Then I broke off and headed for the hotel door. It was a revolving door and I was about to go through it when a Pinkerton stopped me and wanted to know if I were a guest. I told him I was and showed him McKim's key and he waved me on.

The hotel lobby was empty. I went up to the desk clerk and asked him to hold the ledgers for me, not to mention them to anyone else, not to give them to anyone else except the police if I didn't pick them up in an hour. He looked nervous and asked me my name and room number and I took a chance and told him McKim, 418, and he said OK and put the ledgers into his safe.

I took an elevator to the fourth floor and went down the long corridor again. It seemed like I'd gone a mile before I was finally standing just outside the room. My legs were shaking.

The corridor was empty and silent, but I could hear the sound of the TV, muffled by the door. I wondered whether Chip was still in the chair where he'd been when I last saw him or whether he'd gotten sleepy and the redhead had let him bag it on the bed. I tried the key. It went halfway into the lock, then hung up on something. I eased it back out, dipped it into McKim's bottle of glycerin, tried it again. This time it went all the way in without a sound.

I wondered if the chain lock were on. McKim hadn't used it, but I didn't know about the redhead. I took the pistol out of the holster, held it in my right hand with the silencer along-side my cheek. Then, with my left hand, I turned the door-knob as slowly as I could and began to open the door. I'd figured the redhead would be watching TV or looking out the window. I hadn't figured he'd be sitting on the vanity, looking at me as I opened the door, but he was. His wash-blue eyes widened until his eyebrows were lost somewhere behind his bangs. I don't know if he was going for his gun when I shot him. I didn't give a damn. I put a bullet in his chest and watched him sit up a little straighter and then pitch toward the floor.

"Dad!" Chip shouted. He'd been lying on his back on one of the queen-size beds and he came to me and put his arms around me and he was safe and alive and if anything in my life has ever made me happier than that, I don't know what it was.

"Take it easy," I said. "We've got some things to do."

I picked up the ledgers at the desk and we left the hotel. According to the newspapers I'd read, Joseph Nancarrow had been an accountant for the New England Syndicate for 12 years. A month ago, he'd made a deal with the prosecutors, had bought himself immunity in exchange for the financial records McKim and the redhead had gone to so much trouble to steal. It's that kind of world. No use pretending it isn't. I had the ledgers now and I got in touch with the prosecutors and made a deal of my own: a new life for me and for Chip.

My name used to be Hank Gage. It's not Hank Gage anymore. I used to be a manufacturer's rep. I'm not that anymore, either. No chances. No loose ends. That's the only way to fly. I still climb, though. Today Chip and I are going to drive to the high country and do a 1000-foot headwall. It'll take two days. Tonight we'll be snug in our hammocks, hanging from *pitons* a long way up. The wind will blow clean through the high trees. Before we fall asleep, we'll think about the woman who was my wife, each in our own way and without saying anything. At dawn, we'll hear the coyotes bark.

Hey, look, I'm glad I told you about it. Whatever you read in the papers was bull. This is how it happened, just this way. I didn't leave anything out. My son wanted it straight. Oh, yeah. In case you're wondering, he's a little older now. I don't call him Chip anymore.

In the summer of 1961 my wife Nancy and I, with two friends, spent ten days climbing in the San Juan Range of southwestern Colorado. We took the narrow gauge train from Durango to Needleton, then packed twelve miles into a high mountain basin surrounded by thirteen and fourteen thousand foot peaks. This terrain became the setting, in a general way, for "Calloway's Climb" and later for my first novel, Wolf Mountain.

When "Calloway's Climb" first appeared there was a good deal of controversy in climbing circles regarding the scene in which a deceased climber's body is coldbloodedly cut loose from a mountain face. (As I recall, this idea occurred to me after I read an account of a body having been cut loose from an overhang high on the north face of the Eiger.) Some readers felt the scene was unrealistic — others that it was not.

When the story was made into a movie for television several years later, this scene was changed: the climber's body was tied off and left on a ledge, to be retrieved at some later time. I have recently re-read the story, and while I certainly agree the original scene is extremely coldblooded, it still seems to me to be in character with the people whose story this is.

I have also learned that experienced climbers would have no trouble retreating back down a substantial overhang. I considered revising the story to take this into account, but decided not to as I believe Calloway would have pushed for finishing the climb in any case.

Written: Bow Lake, Strafford, New Hampshire;
       Winter, 1973

First Published: *Playboy,* September, 1973

Reprinted: *Playboy,* Italian Edition, September, 1973
       Playboy, German Edition, June, 1974

Recipient of a Martha Foley Award, *Best American Short Stories: 1974* (Houghton Mifflin)

"Calloway's Climb" was dramatized on a one-hour prime-time television movie special starring Mariette Hartley and Patrick O'Neal, with Mike Hoover as "Calloway," in August, 1978. The movie was filmed on location in Yosemite National Park.

CALLOWAY'S CLIMB

The north face of the mountain was still in shadow at mid-morning and the lead boy's yellow parka showed brightly against it as a small and now immobile sun. He stood in web stirrups suspended from *pitons* he had finally managed to drive into the granite roof of an overhang that jutted 15 feet out from a point almost at the perfect center of the steep 2000-foot wall, so that he stood suspended over 1000 feet of space. For two hours, Nils Johnson, a half mile distant at timber line, had watched through his binoculars the agonizing progress of the climb and he knew now, had known for many minutes, that this lead boy was going to fall.

The second boy seemed to know it, too. Less conspicuous in a dark-blue parka, he sat face out, legs dangling from a small ledge 60 feet below and 30 feet west of the center of the over-hang, holding tightly in his gloved hands and across the small of his back the rope that linked him with his companion. Through Johnson's binoculars the rope was a taut golden cable that ran on a bold diagonal up from the second boy's gloved left hand through four equally spaced *pitons,* then through a fifth *piton* driven into a crack in the angle formed by the wall and the overhang. From this final protective *piton,* the rope went out to the waist of the lead boy, around which it had been passed three times and secured with a bowline knot.

The boy continued to stand immobile in his stirrups. His head was close under the roof of the overhang, bent slightly, and he held on to the upper quarter of one of the stirrups with his left hand and kept his balled right fist jammed into a crack that began several feet from the lip of the overhang itself. Occasionally, his companion on the ledge below would crane his neck to follow the diagonal of the golden rope, but he would

not look, Johnson observed, in that direction for long. It was
as if he did not wish to witness the accident that seemed im-
minent, as if he were not sure of the soundness of the *pitons*
the lead boy had placed (and upon which the lead boy's life
would depend in the event of a fall) nor of his own ability to
handle the rope skillfully.

Johnson had two sons, at home in Denver now. His older
son, Tommy, was 12: only a few years younger, he guessed,
than these two boys who for two days had been inching their
way up the steep north face. His wife, Elizabeth, had been the
first to notice them from the camp Johnson had established
beside the clear stream below the first gentle rise of the mountain. It had been his idea, which he had carried out against
her will, to move their camp to the bleak terrain at timber line
from which he might better observe the attempt the boys were
making.

The guidebook evaluated the climb as moderately
difficult, ranging on the decimal system scale from 5.6 to 5.8,
with several pitches, including the central overhang, requir-
ing the direct aid of stirrups and ranging in difficulty from A1
to A2. Johnson remembered it as a long, sometimes arduous
climb, steep and very exposed. When he had done it a decade
earlier, it had been customary to allow two days for the ascent, bivouacking on the area above the overhang; but in the
years since then, numerous ropes of two had completed the
wall in a single day.

The two boys who were attempting the climb now had
not managed to reach the overhang in their first day, had spent
what Johnson knew must have been a miserably uncomfortable night on the small ledge from which the boy in blue now
payed out the rope. He had guessed from the poor time they
were making, their long delays and awkward movements on
the wall, that they were too inexperienced, too wary to succeed; and he had been surprised this morning when, instead
of roping down the face, they had prepared to climb the over-

hang, which, once passed, would cut off their retreat. The first 1000 feet of the wall were the least complex, the central over-hang was a reasonably straightforward technical problem, and it was only in the final 1000 feet that the climb became rigorous in its demands.

Johnson put the binoculars in his lap for a moment, closed his eyes, realigned his back against a rough concavity of sun-warmed stone behind him. He thought he knew what that lead boy was feeling; how he had reached or nearly reached the limits of skill and, perhaps, of nerve; how his ability to act, to go on or go back, was suspended now as he was suspend-ed over 1000 feet of space; how a seven-sixteenths-inch-diameter rope, passing as it did through a handful of *pitons,* was his umbilical link with his companion, upon whose courage and skill as belayer his life would depend, should he fall in what would have to be his attempt, finally, to advance or retreat.

I should have gotten my butt over there, Johnson thought. *I might have been able to call them down.*

But she, whose bitterness, like a stream that had run deep underground for years and had begun to rise and threaten the surface of their life together, would, he knew, have used his concern for the boys against him, would have managed to manipulate it toward something sentimental with which she then would gently mock him as one more coupon torn from her book of payment for what had been his recent and disap-pointing infidelities.

He'll make a move out of his stirrups. He'll try to clear the over-hang, but he's much too far back. If he does fall, and that last pi-ton pulls, or his friend panics, or the belay is rigged poorly. . . .

Then he knew she was coming to join him, heard her de-liberately clumsy-footed approach as she came up across the rock-strewn slope from the last line of stunted firs beside which he had stubbornly carried out last night his erecting of their tent. Aware he admired grace, she kicked stones from her path with the toes of her climbing shoes, stood over him finally, looking down, her face even more attractive in its maturity, he thought, than it had been when, years ago now, he had been a young, cocksure instructor of English, and she, with an impassivity that had captured him, had led half a stadium in cheers for the Colorado football team. She wore her high-cut faded Levi shorts and scarlet long-sleeved jersey well, for she had scrupulously maintained her figure and even through her pregnancies had gained so little weight that Johnson had wondered since if this might account for the slightness of his sons. Her brown hair was long: She had arranged it this morning into a ponytail that spilled across her left shoulder, down the front of her jersey almost to her waist. She had, in recent months, left off wearing a bra, an emblem, he knew, of her liberation not from men in general — she had not yet pursued her instincts that far — but from him in particular. Her breasts were well shaped, but her nipples were large and it embarrassed him to see where they jutted against the fabric of her shirt.

"I thought we had a date this morning," she said. Her voice was pleasant and only one long familiar with it would have detected the slight vehicle of contempt upon which it rode.

"I was worried about those boys," he replied. He made an effort to stand.

"Don't get up," she told him. "I'd like to sit in the sun for a while. It hasn't managed to reach the tent."

"Did you warm up the eggs?"

"I ate them cold. Your fire was out." In recent months, she had become deft with the apparently innocuous phrase, and this both amused and troubled him, for until now, the ironies of their relationship had been his to define.

"Look," he said. He handed her the binoculars. With a studied lack of interest, she took them, making the adjustments necessary to adapt the lenses to her perfect sight.

"So?"

"So he's been there too long. Almost half an hour."

"Maybe he's resting."

"I don't think so."

"Well," she said, laughing as she returned the glasses. "What do you want to do – go up and bring him down in your weight-trained arms?"

"It won't be funny if he falls."

"I wasn't implying that it would."

"I don't think the other boy is very well experienced: He handles the rope awkwardly."

"Really."

"Look, if all you can do is be bitchy," he bristled, "why don't you go back to the tent?"

"Because, Nils, I've been in the tent all morning." Then, as if sensing that he could become angry and end by his silence her pleasure in tormenting him, she added: "Somebody's taken the place we had by the stream."

"Oh?" he said. "Who?"

"I haven't the slightest idea. I saw the smoke from his fire this morning. He has a small blue tent, an orange parka and moves nicely. I think he's alone."

"Is he a climber?"

"I don't know."

"Are you sure he's alone?"

"Yes. Quite."

This range of mountains was remote and the season was still early, but the area was popular with climbers and Johnson, who had come here in what had proved so far a futile effort to mend his relationship with her and – though he had not told her this – to revisit scenes of his earlier and more successful climbing days, was not surprised that others had come here, too. He wore new steel-rimmed spectacles, a stylish departure from his customary horn-rims. When he raised the binoculars now, he found they had lost clarity from her adjustments and he had to make adjustments of his own.

The lead boy, he observed finally, had driven yet another *piton* into the roof of the overhang, close to its outer edge, had clipped a stirrup into it and was testing the integrity of this stirrup now with his right hand, yanking its webbing back and forth. Then, slowly and awkwardly, he transferred his weight from the first and second of the web stirrups to the second and third.

"Good." Johnson breathed hard. "Good. Now you've got it. Now get up and over before you lose your nerve."

"Is that what happened to you this morning?" she asked lightly.

"Betts, I told you; I was worried about them."

"Wouldn't it be better to assume they know what they're doing?"

"I don't think they do know."

"We were going to make love, I think," she said. "Then have breakfast."

She pulled the jersey over her head, folded it and put it on the rough ground beside her.

"Do you think that's smart if other people are around?" he remarked.

"Don't tell me you care."

"Don't you?"

"Not really. No."

He glanced instinctively in the direction from which the stranger she had mentioned might appear.

"You used to be modest," he said. "I remember that from the start. When we had our first apartment, that depressing place downtown, I'd tell you to take things off during the day, remember that? And you wouldn't do it. You used to get angry as hell."

"I've changed. I'd do it now, but you don't ask."

"I still like the way you look. You know that. It's just been so bloody long—"

"I know what you're going to say," she said. "All of your

clever arguments about the value of fucking around, and I really don't want to hear them again, all right?"

He sighed. "I thought we were going to try to do better, by getting away. . . ."

"So did I. But it's been a big nothing so far."

"Were you willing to let it be anything else?"

"I don't know. Maybe not. But I think I was willing to try last night, and again this morning, if you had stayed around, if you'd been half as keen about me as you were about those damn boys."

He started to defend himself, but his position seemed hopeless and he lay back against the concavity of stone. She knelt before him, aware, he knew, that the sight of her familiar breasts unconcealed in this new environment could still arouse him.

"I'm not one of your pretty coeds," she said. "But I do feel like screwing—according to Plan A of our reconciliation—and as far as I know, except for whoever that is by the stream, you're the only man around."

"Well, go ahead, then," he said. "Help yourself."

"Thank you, Nils. I'll do that. Just try to be up to it, all right?"

"I usually am, aren't I?"

"Oh, yes. You're very big in the erection department."

He could not help laughing, but she was not amused and prepared him with a masculine detachment that, along with her coarseness, was not characteristic of her.

"Whatever you think, I still love you," he tried to say, touched by this sentiment as she arranged herself over him.

"That's not a very big deal for me right now."

"I've said I was sorry. I've told you it was an empty, meaningless thing; that it didn't work out."

"I've heard that before."

"Well, why don't you pay me back, then? So we can forget it and be civil again? Why don't you have an affair of your own?"

"Maybe I will, Nils."

"I think it would make a lot of sense. I really do." He had argued endlessly with her that they should accept what had become the new morality: relieve themselves of some of the burdens of a confining and fixed relationship, with its absurd prerogative of jealousy. He had buttressed his persuasions with his customary and careful logic, but she had surrendered nothing to him, and his own attempts to enter a more exciting life that seemed increasingly to be passing them by had failed so far partly, he knew, because of her stubborn refusal to join him, at least in spirit. In this way, it had come to pass that he lived in a state of perpetual agitation that he had with wretched poor luck been born, as he saw it, a decade too soon.

"My students tell me that marriage is quaint," he said.

"Keep still, will you," she told him. Halfheartedly, he took her breasts in his hands. He felt too exposed here on this open upslope of rock and was distracted by the possibility that the man who was camped by the stream might wander up this way and find them copulating. The concern surprised him, for he had not suspected until now that in such matters he might be shy; he could not remember that they had ever made love in the open before.

"*Jesus,*" she said. She was moving rapidly now.

Gently, he put his hands on her.

"*God, I hate you,*" she said. "*I hate you, Nils.*"

She had begun the first of her cries when beyond the arc of her shoulder, through the sweet strands of her hair that moved in a soft breeze (as clearly as if his vision were still somehow aided but no longer magnified by the binoculars), a tiny yellow dot began its fall from the near center of the vast north face of the mountain. It fell spasmodically as, in succession, each of the *pitons* held for a second or two, then sprang from the cracks into which they had been driven, the tiny yellow dot swinging finally like the pendulum of a clock back and forth across the wall until, after what seemed a long time, it hung motionless by a golden thread about 70 feet below the ledge upon which, Johnson knew, a boy in a dark-blue parka held whatever was left of the life of his friend, desperately, in his two gloved hands.

"*Betts,*" he whispered in fright as she relaxed at last against him. "*That lead boy fell.*"

She had wanted to go at once for the assistance of the man who had taken their campsite by the stream but Johnson had argued against it. Now, scarcely three hours later and already 400 feet up the standard north-face route, he was confident his decision had been best, that an hour or more could have been lost in attracting the help of a man neither he nor Elizabeth could be sure was a mountaineer. He moved up yet another lead toward the two boys. The boy in blue was still seated on the ledge, facing out, holding the rope in his hands, across the small of his back; the rope plunged over the edge of the ledge, taut to the place where, about 70 feet below, the boy in yellow was suspended from it as motionless as if he had been hanged. Johnson reflected that, in addition to the incessant, throbbing anxiety he felt for these young boys, he also felt a guilty pride in his ability – even after the erosion of years – to manage such a difficult climb. And he felt, too, a relief, surprising in its intensity, that he and the woman he had married were joined by the rope now as they so often had been in their early years together, he leading the way, she climbing second behind him.

The sun was on the wall, but the rock under Johnson's hands still felt cool; a warm, westerly breeze gentled against the right side of his face. He made his moves precisely and out of 20 years' experience, studying through his steel-rimmed spectacles that portion of the route that lay directly above him, finding and testing his holds, balancing up from one to the next, placing his *pitons* with care and at somewhat longer intervals than he would have liked, for he had not expected to do this extensive a climb and had packed in only a small amount of gear.

She stood easily on her belay stance 100 feet below him now, anchored to the wall, paying the rope to him as he climbed. Unlike him, she had never been afraid of high places, had never had to overcome the kind of terror he had felt in his first year. Since they had begun their ascent to assist the two boys, she had sustained an attitude toward him that was crisp, efficient and yielded nothing of what he hoped might be her willingness to forget, at least for a while, what had been their recent past.

"Twenty feet!" he heard her call.

"All right!" he answered. His heart beat rapidly.

He had given up calling to the boy in blue above him. Either he had been too stunned by the accident or his mouth was too cotton dry to answer. Apparently, he had not tied the rope off to the anchor *piton* behind him as he should have done by now in order to free his hands. Johnson knew how terrible that weight could be and wondered if the belay had been rigged properly: In whatever fashion it had been rigged, at least it had held; but the boy in yellow had showed no sign of consciousness and Johnson was reluctant to think what that might mean. Although he had participated in many rescues, seen numerous deaths, he had never managed to quite make his own attitude one of protective fatalism that most of his colleagues shared, that was also shared by Elizabeth, whose toughness he had often envied.

He found a suitable position on the wall, anchored himself and turned to face out. From here he could see the falling blue-green forested slope of the mountain and the distant glinting meander of the stream; could watch now, and take in the rope, as she climbed toward him.

She was a natural, a born climber, and he knew if she had spent a fraction of the time he had in perfecting skills, she might have been better than he. He could not help feeling proud of her as he watched her make her careful, efficient moves toward him. It was as if now in their absence of affection, she had become a finely crafted instrument that he had been wise enough, lucky enough, to purchase at a time when the demand for her had been superficial and his own credit had been good. Pausing just long enough to retrieve the *pitons* he had driven, whacking them loose from their cracks with her hammer, clipping them and their carabiners smartly to a loop of rope she had draped from her right shoulder to her left hip across the scarlet jersey she wore, she would glance up along the route, choosing her holds, her quick perceptive eyes never quite meeting his own.

"You're climbing beautifully," he said when she reached him.

"How much longer will it take?"

"I don't know. A couple of hours, maybe. We're making good time."

"Has he moved at all?" she asked, squinting up.

"No."

"What about the other one?"

"I can't get him to answer. He's probably scared to death."

"We haven't got enough ropes to get them down, do we?"

"We'll rig something."

He had hoped, as they switched positions now, moving gingerly on the steep wall, she might return his compliment; but she was silent and he adjusted the rope where it circled his waist, shifted impatiently the sweat-stained straps of the small red rucksack he carried and into which he had put some sandwiches and candy bars, their first-aid kit and extra clothing.

"Want something to eat?"

"I can wait," she said.

"How about some water?"

"No, thank you."

He put his hand on hers where she held the rope in readiness to pay out to him as he went.

"Betts," he started to say. She looked at him. Her eyes were green and they pooled now with tears.

"Don't," she whispered.

"I just wanted to say thanks for doing this with me. I couldn't have done it alone." And he added, painfully aware that he meant it: "There's no one I'd rather be up here with. Do you believe that?"

She shook her head.

"Don't do this, Nils," she said. "Those boys need our help. If you're ready to go, you better go."

He felt angry that he had opened himself to her and a need now to be cruel.

"All right, fine," he said, already beginning to climb. "Try not to cry, will you, because if you do cry, you'll have trouble handling the rope."

"Don't worry about how I handle the rope," she replied, as if he were no longer a central fact of her life, no longer worthy of her anger. "Look," she said. "There he is."

"What?" he grumbled. "There who is?"

"The one I told you about. The one who took our place by the stream."

He glanced over his shoulder and down. Five hundred feet below the place where he stood balanced now on two small outcroppings of rock, a lone figure in an orange parka waved up: a figure that had materialized, it seemed, out of a void. Johnson blinked. A speck under his left eyelid had troubled him since he and Elizabeth had made love.

"Is he a climber?" he asked, moving up again. He had not bothered to return the wave.

"Yes, I think so. He's got a rope."

"Well, that's not going to do us much good, is it?" he said.

"It could," she said.

"What's that supposed to mean?"

She was silent for a moment and Johnson, in an awkward position on the wall, his confidence threatened subtly by the fact that now, as he climbed, he was being observed, swore softly.

"Give me some slack, will you?" he said. "What do you mean, it could?" Then he heard her laugh, as if she were relieved, as if her instincts about the stranger had been correct.

"Nils, he's coming up," she said. "By himself."

The afternoon breeze gentled finally along the surfaces of the range and higher winds began to fill the visible sky with cloud. The lead boy's body, which had bumped against the wall while the breeze had been strong, now hung motionless again from the rope, which had been jerked by the fall from his waist to a point just under his arms. On the belaying ledge, some 70 feet higher, the other boy's legs dangled and were also motionless except when, from time to time, he would bang his boots together as if to restore circulation, creating as he did an alien, helpless sound. Johnson heard it as he stood with his wife, together now on a small ledge 200 feet below the body of the fallen boy, watching as the stranger made his lone ascent.

"He's over halfway," she said, peering intently down. "He's fantastic."

Grudgingly, Johnson agreed, aware that at the rate this stranger was moving up, unencumbered as he was by a second, by *piton*craft and belay, he would very likely reach them before they reached the boys. He climbed almost jauntily, his orange parka tied around his waist, a small green lump of a pack bouncing against the back of what looked from Johnson's perspective like a white dress shirt with the sleeves rolled up, its tails tucked into a pair of combat trousers. He carried a coil of rope over his shoulder and had a way of leaning out from the nearly vertical wall, studying the route for a while, then making half a dozen consecutive moves, some of which would carry him as far as 15 or 20 feet at a time. In his own history as a climber, Johnson had seen no more than a handful of men who moved as well as this man moved, and none that he could

remember who had moved any better. It was a performance
he respected and envied, for in it was written a talent that he
himself had never had; and while he was relieved that he
would now have this standard of help in carrying out the res-
cue, he could not quite put aside a sense of threat that seemed
for him to emanate from the simple fact of this man with
whom he had not as yet exchanged a word and for whom his
wife had expressed a frank, even provocative regard.

"Has anyone ever soloed this face before?" she asked.

"No, I don't think so. I haven't heard of anybody."

"You must know who he is; he's not just anybody."

Johnson wiped his spectacles, which, during his hours on
the wall, had become covered with a pumiceous dust.

"I don't recognize him. There are plenty like him these days."

"We're lucky to have him," she said.

"And his rope."

"Of course, Nils. His rope, too."

Johnson went up another 100-foot lead, moving with conscious deliberation, as if, in what had become an atmospheric intensity, he might otherwise be impetuous. He brushed his
handholds free of grit, settled his fingers onto them, tested his
footholds fussily with the rigid soles of his *Kletterschuhe.* He
balanced carefully up in clean motions, assuring himself by
the care he was taking that he would not be embarrassed by
a fall. Then he found a good stance, a deep, cavelike pocket
in the rock from which he could belay comfortably, and leaning against the stone behind him, sitting with his legs straight
out, he brought in the slack rope and called for her to join him.
Halfway through the pitch, she had trouble removing one of
his *pitons.* He could hear her banging it stubbornly with her
hammer and, when he leaned awkwardly out from his position, he could see her small hand clenched around the
carabiner, yanking it fitfully back and forth.

"Leave it, why don't you?" he called. Scarcely 100 feet below her, the lone man was coming up, moving swiftly now,

for here the face was somewhat less steep and offered a variety of holds.

"I'm going to get the goddamned thing," he heard her say. "Give me some tension, will you?"

He took up the slight belly of slack that had developed between them until the rope was taut and she could use both of her hands in her attempt to loosen the jammed *piton*. Finally, with an odd sense of relief, as if it had been driven into his own heart, he heard it spring free, heard her snap it to the collection that hung from her shoulder loop.

"All right, climbing," she called.

"Climb ahead," he said.

The north face was in shadow again, the air cool out of the sun; he had a sense that dusk would come rapidly and that rain would fall. A swallow swept by the place where he sat; he heard the subdued jetlike hiss of its passing. He was hungry and quite tired now and knew before he could begin the next and final lead the lone man would reach this place.

That lead boy is dead, he thought. *I'm sure of it.*

When she reached him, her familiar face rising suddenly in front of the opening of the recess in which he sat, he drew his knees to his chest in order to make room for her; but instead of changing places with him, as he had expected her to, she kept her position on the steep wall, turning, resting an arm along the threshold of the recess and, in doing this, whether deliberately he could not tell, she blocked his egress from the cave.

"I'm ready to climb," he told her.

"Let me rest a minute, Nils," she said tiredly. "I wore out my arm pulling that damn *piton*."

"You should have left it. We've been doing fine; we've got enough to finish."

"It always seems like a defeat to me to leave one. Hi," she said. She was looking down and had, apparently, spoken to the man who was coming up from somewhere below her.

Johnson guessed from the little volume she had used that the man must be close now, and there had been a shyness in her tone that he recognized but had not heard her use in a long time. He caught the distant jingling of the *pitons* and carabiners the man carried, but as yet had not used, and heard his reply, friendly, he thought, but muffled to incoherence by the cave. Johnson moved restlessly, sensing what would be his disadvantage if the man suddenly arrived.

"Come on, Betty," he said.

"I don't know," she said, not speaking to him but to the one who was coming up. "Yes," she said. "I know. My husband saw the fall."

Then the man was standing next to her, keeping his easy balance with a careless touch of his hand to the outside edge of one of the walls of the recess, looking in to the denlike place where Johnson sat. He was a young man, mid-20s, Johnson guessed, and though he had been climbing steadily for a long time now, he showed no evident signs of fatigue. His hair was wavy and brown, fashionable in its length but also, Johnson observed, professionally trimmed. His strength was evident in his hands and wrists and forearms where they showed below the rolled-back sleeves of his shirt; and in his blue eyes, his friendly but unyielding expression, across the tanned surfaces and well-shaped planes of his face, Johnson thought he read privilege: private schools, perhaps, trips abroad, easy and useful connections in high places; and these assumptions seemed to gain validity as, when the young man spoke, his tones warm yet at the same time sober and carrying with them the confidence of one who has not only managed to survive his life so far but also managed to prevail in it, Johnson caught the cultivated accents of the East.

"Hi," he said. "My name's Calloway."

And before Johnson could reply, the young man added, as if they had all just met on the approach to a tee on a busy golf course: "Do you mind if I go by?"

The lead boy, in fact, was dead. It appeared he had died instantly in his fall, his neck broken, his blond head jutting unnaturally above the bright color of his parka, a weal of blood congealed at one corner of his mouth. Calloway was removing the equipment the boy had carried, adding it impatiently to his own as if it might prove useful—the *pitons,* carabiners, web stirrups, and slings—as Johnson came up, belayed by Elizabeth some 90 feet below now in the cave. The sky had darkened with cloud, the air was quite still; already, he had heard thunder.

"How's the other one?" he asked, pausing tentatively on his holds, for he had seen Calloway climb up to the ledge.

"Psyched out. He won't say anything. I tied the rope off for him."

"Does he know about this?"

"I told him," Calloway said. "I don't know if it registered."

Gnats were moving near the dead boy's eyes. Johnson looked away. The meander of the stream was lost in distant shadow now. Soon, he knew, a breeze would rise; almost surely, the late-afternoon rain would come. Below, he saw Elizabeth lean out from the cave, look up, her face a pale, expectant wedge above the fabric of her jersey. He shook his head. She would be saddened, he knew, but not surprised: Though she had not said so, he thought she had intuited from the beginning that the boy had not survived his fall.

"We don't have enough daylight left to get the other one down," Johnson said. "Even if we get lucky and the storm misses us."

Calloway agreed. He seemed to be waiting for the older man to make a decision, perhaps out of deference to his age, perhaps because he had been first on the wall. Johnson, keeping one hand on the rock, removed his spectacles, wiped his brow with the sleeve of his shirt. The urgency of reaching this place had given him an adrenal strength that now was rapid-

ly ebbing away as if to follow what had been his last fragile
hope for the fallen boy. Tired, hungry, balanced gingerly on
his holds, he felt his legs begin to shake; slight cramps had developed in the lower muscles of his calves.

Calloway looked up in the direction of the summit that
towered above them, merging now into what had become a
granite-colored sky. He seemed disgruntled, impatient to be
on his way, to separate himself from this death and the failure
of which it spoke. When he brushed back a shock of his brown
hair and looked intently at Johnson again, Johnson sensed the
younger man had reached the far limits of whatever refine-
ment had prevented him so far from simply taking charge: and
even out of his exhaustion and reluctance to state a position
the younger man might challenge, Johnson discovered in himself a need to preserve his place.

"We'll have to bivouac," he said.

"Right."

"There's room on that ledge for two —"

"I think we should do the overhang." Calloway cut in —
and it was clear he had worked it out, was sure of himself. "According to the book, that's the standard site. There's room
enough up there for six."

"We'd be burning our bridges —"

"We can go on up and finish the face in the morning."

"I don't know," Johnson said.

"I've read the route description," Calloway said. "It doesn't
sound bad; I'm frankly not worried about it. We can go one
rope of four or two ropes of two; whichever you like. Once
we're up there, we can walk down the east ridge. No problem.

"Look," he said. "There's no point in spending a rotten night."

"Do you think that other boy will be up to doing the
overhang?"

"He'll do what we tell him to do," Calloway said. "What
about this one? We'll need the rope. We can tie him off here
or cut him loose."

Johnson poked a finger to his eye where, under the lid, a speck still burned. The younger man had spoken without feeling, and it was not so much this fact that troubled Johnson (he understood it as a logical and useful attitude to hold) but the fact that he could not quite do the same, that when he spoke he knew he would hear along the edges of his voice traces of the pulse of loss he felt.

"I guess there's not much point in tying him off," he said finally. "Not if we're going on. One of us should be up there with the other one, though."

"Go ahead," Calloway said. He seemed more relaxed now that they had reached a decision. "I'll take care of it. What about your wife? Will it bother her?"

"She won't like it, but she's been through this kind of thing before. She'll be all right."

"She's lovely," Calloway said. He had fished a clasp knife from his pocket. Johnson watched as the younger man drew the long blade out with the disk of his nail. The compliment had struck him as gratuitous and he did not respond to it.

"Give me a couple of minutes up there," he said. Then, as he turned to climb, he realized he would not have enough rope to reach the ledge. Calloway saw the problem at once.

"I'll give you a belay," he said. Folding the blade back into its handle, he returned the knife to his pocket and began to uncoil his rope. Johnson could not help feeling a little embarrassed, Calloway having so recently climbed unprotected to the same ledge. He called to Elizabeth, told her the plan, and then, the belay established, Calloway paying out rope from an easy, slouching stance, he went up.

The surviving boy sat on the ledge, in his blue parka, gazing vacantly out. His hands were placed on his lap in such a way that Johnson could see where the rope, during his efforts to stop the fall, had scorched the leather of the palms. He was a red-haired, freckled boy, and Johnson tried talking to him, tried to comfort him as best he could, but the boy would not speak, only nodded his head or shook it or simply gazed out at the visible horizon of high mountains and dark, lightning-illuminated cloud.

The ledge was rough, even smaller than Johnson had remembered. When he removed his pack and sat next to the boy, he felt their shoulders touch. The rope, anchored to the wall behind them, bent sharply over the edge of the shelf; and although Johnson did not wish to look at it, he forced himself to, watched it unblinkingly until, suddenly freed of its burden, it sprang lightly up. He wondered then how long it would take for the body to fall and whether or not the sound of it striking the earth might be heard at a vertical distance of almost 1000 feet. He felt an oppressive sense of inevitability. Removing his spectacles, closing his eyes for a moment, he was grateful for what had become a remote yet persistent rumble of thunder.

"I'm sorry about your friend," he said quietly, repeating what he had said before.

"He's my stepbrother," the boy said. And during the time it took for the others to come up, and even after that, these were the only words he spoke.

In reduced light, from a standing belay position established by Calloway just below the ledge, Elizabeth payed out rope to the younger man as he climbed on a bold diagonal to the overhang and then, with astonishing swiftness, built a near catwalk of stirrups from the wall to its outer lip. He trailed the belay rope behind him as if it were nothing more than an obligation, and when he stood in the last of the stirrups, his left fist balled into a crack at the edge of the overhang, he leaned out and peered up in what had become his familiar reconnaissance of route, and then, without hesitation once he had hauled up a great belly of slack so as not to be impeded by the rope behind him, he reached up with his right hand, kicked his foot free of the last stirrup, swung out over 1000 feet of

space, hung there for a fraction of a second, then went cleanly up and over.

Johnson shook his head. He looked at Elizabeth, saw
across the pale, tired planes of her face her frank regard for
what Calloway had done. It would be easy for the rest of them
to follow, protected from above by the young man whose confident cry of "Climb!" they heard already come indistinctly
down.

Elizabeth went first, moving surely to the overhang itself,
pausing, then going out from stirrup to stirrup until she stood
in the last stirrup and Johnson, who sat on the small rough
ledge, belaying her from behind, felt a clutch of fear as he saw
this woman who had been his companion through all his adult
years and who was the mother of his sons poised in a place
almost identical to that where the lead boy had stood just prior
to his fall; and when Johnson heard her familiar voice call for
tension on the upper rope and saw her scrabble finally up and
safely out of sight, he felt such relief as to make him weak,
and he sighed and wiped his face.

"Go ahead," he said hoarsely to the surviving boy, once the
ropes were secured. The boy was brave, possessed of a courage
not buttressed by experience or any special skill. He went awkwardly up and out and over, his wash-blue eyes still trauma-
tized with shock, his legs shaking badly all the while he stood
in the stirrups under the dusky overhang, his hands stutter-
ing from hold to hold, trailing obediently behind him the rope
from which less than one hour ago the body of his stepbrother
had been cut away.

Wearily, Johnson stood. His own legs were unsteady, his
shoulders sore where the straps of his pack had chafed them.
By the time he had knotted the rope around his waist and
ascended to the overhang, the sky had grown so dark he had
to wait for flashes of lightning in order to see clearly the ghost-
white webbing of the stirrups that advanced outward from the
cliff, appearing now as if they had been driven into something

as insubstantial as the air itself that eddied indecisively against the face, agitated by what he guessed would prove a quick rising of the wind.

He moved cautiously from stirrup to stirrup, taking them and their carabiners with him as he went, hearing the clink and jingle of the metal as it collected around him, sensing through his finger tips the building charge of atmospheric electricity, straining his ears to hear the warning buzz, hearing only the still-distant roll of thunder, calling to Calloway for tension at last, feeling the rope pull swiftly and hard against him, hoping briefly that it would, in fact, hold him as he let it take his weight, leaned back against it out over the dark void, its engulfing dimensions clear only in the flashes of lightning that would illuminate the sky and earth for several seconds now before they flickered out and the artillery of thunder would boom along the distant range; reaching awkwardly in under the overhang to unclip the last of the stirrups, groping tiredly for some purchase on the sharp-edged rock as, from above, Calloway applied his strength to the rope; kicking and thrashing until at last he managed to deliver himself in the absence of all grace to the abundant area above the overhang where Elizabeth sat next to the younger man, combing out her long brown hair as if she were at the dressing table in the bedroom of their Denver home, and the surviving boy gazed vacantly out, and Calloway popped up and stretched and said, in his cultivated accents: "Good show. Fine. Now let's eat."

For a while, the lightning played along the far peaks, then the storm collected itself and moved off into the east, leaving behind its unfulfilled promise of rain and the light of a luminous moon. The temperature of the air began to drop, and by the time they had eaten their rations of food and Calloway had brewed tea for them all on the small Primus stove he had fished from his pack, the surfaces of the rock around them were damp to touch. Elizabeth sat next to the younger man

in the area of what had become their kitchen. Johnson, separated from her by the surviving boy, watched as she applied
fresh lipstick, a rust red he knew, close in color to that of the
parka she now wore. He could read nothing in this old and
feminine gesture except her habit of paying attention to her
appearance wherever she happened to be; and yet when she
pulled her lips together and recapped the small gold tube, he
was surprised by a desire to have her sit next to him and sensed
at the same time how awkward it might be to change positions,
how she, or even Calloway, might be amused. Briefly, out of
some as-yet-indistinct kinship of soul, he put his hand on the
knob of the surviving boy's knee.

"How are you doing?" he said.

"OK," the boy replied, but he was half-hearted.

"We were lucky we missed the rain."

"I know."

"My name is Nils," he said. "What's yours?"

"Perry."

"Where do you live?"

"Durango."

"Have you done much climbing before this?"

"No."

Johnson nodded. Over the hiss of the stove he could hear the
others talking. They talked easily, as if instead of just having
met during this encounter on the wall, they had known and liked
each other awhile. In his relationship with Elizabeth, played as
it had been until now to the beat of his own drum, he had never
experienced anything more than the most innocuous sort of
jealousy. She had been so doggedly loyal to him that he had more
than once in the privacy of his thoughts charged against her a
lack of imagination. Now, in the context of her recent efforts
to assert herself and the presence of this young, able and mag-
netic man, he felt a rising threat and she, whom he had taken
quite for granted these many years, seemed to become more
desirable, even precious, as she moved in spirit away from him.

Later, when Calloway suggested to him they begin next morning in two ropes of two, Johnson, his own practical judgement arguing against it, found that he had agreed. A consecutive rope of four with Calloway in the lead would, in spite of its slowness, he thought, be almost perfectly safe. But the younger man had made his suggestion in such a way as to cast no doubt upon Johnson's ability to lead his own rope; and, therefore, to argue against the suggestion once it had been made would have been, it seemed to Johnson, a confession of inadequacy. In spite of his fatigue, he thought he had climbed well in the first 1000 feet and was reasonably confident that he and Elizabeth could manage to complete the wall, if not with Calloway's finesse, at least with competence. It was only after a general agreement to proceed in two ropes of two that the surviving boy, for the first time, ventured a comment of his own.

"Can I go with you?" he asked Johnson, his voice still unsteady but loud enough for the others to hear.

"Fine," Calloway said at once, as if he sensed the boy did not quite trust him. "Elizabeth and I will lead. We'll take the spare rope. If there's any problem, we can all join up."

"Is that all right with you, Nils?" he heard her ask.

"Sure. Fine," he said. But he felt as if in a game of chess he had been tempted by his opponent into making a move the consequences of which he could not quite anticipate; and he wondered if his voice had betrayed his uncertainty.

Three of them lay down then and tried to sleep in their respective places on the ledge. The last thing Johnson remembered seeing was the silhouette of Calloway, who continued to sit cross-legged, gazing out where the moon rose, sipping his tea.

It went well in the first 400 feet. Then, perhaps no longer concerned, Calloway and Elizabeth began to move ahead. At 500 feet above the bivouac ledge, they were one full lead beyond Johnson and the boy; at 600 feet above the ledge, they

were no longer in sight. An early wind had risen in the north-
east and was blowing hard against the face. The surfaces of
the rocks were cold to touch.

Johnson blew on his finger tips, squinted through his spectacles at the route above. He had reached a difficult section
and was having trouble making his moves. He guessed the angle of the rock to be 80 degrees here, the small holds it provided
infrequent and awkwardly distributed, so that twice he had
found the only way he could shift his position and advance
was to move down several inches and then reascend, placing
his left foot where his right had been. He had tried to protect
himself as well as he could, but the wall here was smooth and
the few cracks it provided were shallow and he had used up
all of his smaller *pitons.* Eighty feet below, anchored to the wall
and belaying from stirrups, the surviving boy handled the rope
indifferently, as if to him it was not conceivable that a man
like Johnson could fall.

He closed his eyes, pressed his cheek against the rock.
Transmitted through it he could hear the remote sound, no
louder than the ticking of his watch, of Calloway banging a
piton somewhere into the face above. He wanted to call for
help, his pride would have allowed for that, but he knew he
would not be heard in this wind and at this distance, knew
if he did call he would alert the boy below to the fact they were
in trouble, and that could only make things worse.

He looked up, hoping to catch a glimpse of the others, but
where the wall tilted toward a less acute angle, he saw only
a blue sky full of racing cloud, which, in this perspective, gave
him the giddy sense that the mountain itself was toppling forward. Elizabeth had left *pitons* in all the most difficult pitches
so far and here, 15 feet above the reach of his hand, he could
see two web stirrups tossing like bunting in the wind. To reach
these stirrups, he would have to negotiate a section of rock
that appeared so steep and generally faultless and barren of
holds he could not imagine how Calloway had done it, or he

himself had done it a decade earlier, as he must have, though he held no specific memory.

He hugged the wall, felt its harshness against him. He lifted his right foot to a nubbin, slowly let it begin to take his weight, moving up an inch at a time, searching with his left hand, finding a shallow striation into which he could place the pads of his finger tips. His heart beat rapidly. When he made his next delicate move up, he felt the rope tug at his waist, and he angrily called for slack and felt the pressure ease slowly and then saw the rope belly out on the wall below his right foot and knew the boy, who had previously given him too little, now was giving him too much, but he was hoarse and more afraid than he had been since his first years as a climber, and so, without trying to communicate any further with the boy, he committed himself to yet another slight move up this sheerness of rock, found at last a thin crack with his right hand, jammed his fingers in to the second joints, felt the skin rip away, the pulse of blood, a terrible relief to have gotten even this much purchase here, moved his left foot then to a nutlike nubbin of rock scarcely large enough to take the extreme edge of his shoe, felt the wind hurling itself against him as if to dislodge him, heard it wail and sigh in the large pockets and crevices above, saw the rope belly out along the wall below, as if the surviving boy had simply payed out all the slack he had and was waiting passively for this pitch to be over.

Johnson swore, felt a sudden brutal anger that she had left him here alone, had climbed on out of sight and sound with Calloway, who must have passed this way without effort. Why had she not waited as had been their plan? Why had she not left a solid *piton,* thought of him, remembered him? He closed his eyes against the wind, guessed in the irrationality of his anger and fear that she would be Calloway's now, and then someone else's, and someone else's after that. He knew how it went, how insubstantial a bond fidelity was once it had been breached a single time and knew for the first time, felt, even, how she must have felt: the humiliation, old, ancient, of the one betrayed.

He opened his eyes, swore. He was in a half-crouched position now, his right arm stretched at full length above him, his right hand jammed in the thin crack, his left hand flat against the wall, his right foot scraping uselessly, his left leg trembling as he let it take his weight and began to rise out of his half crouch, pushing down on his left foot, pulling up with his right hand; and he had drawn himself to almost a full standing position when the nutlike nubbin broke suddenly and cleanly away under his left foot and he fell abruptly, the right side of his face scraping along the wall, his spectacles tugging up from his ears, bobbling, his left hand flashing up too late to stop them as they swept away from him, buffeted and joggled by the wind to fall the 1600 feet to the ground above which he hung suspended now by the fingers of his right hand, his inarticulate cry cut off by the clutching dryness of his throat. Vision blurred, he felt the strength ebb quickly from his arm, and just as quickly, in what was left of the time he would have, he began to pull himself up, testing the wall with the edges of his shoes until he found at last a small lip that would take his weight, and he balanced gingerly up until he stood pressed flat, his face close to the bloody fingers that had saved him. Then, for five long minutes, with the wind slamming against him, its banshee sound in his ears, he did nothing more or less than breathe.

The crack was shallow. It took just over two inches of the six-inch *piton* he drove, but that much of it was tightly wedged and when he slipped a loop of rope over it, down the exposed shaft of the *piton* to the place where the *piton* entered the crack, and clipped a stirrup onto that loop of rope, the stirrup held his weight and enabled him then to step up slowly and reach the stirrups she had left, and from that point forward, the wall was pleasant again and he and the boy finished it without incident.

Elizabeth and Calloway were waiting at the summit, sitting together in the lee of an upthrust slab of rock.

"Hello, Nils," she said offhandedly. But then she noticed the blood on his hand and the fact that he was not wearing his glasses and she seemed concerned, he thought, when she asked him what had happened.

"I was in the middle of a scramble," he told her. "The wind took them."

"Are you all right?"

"Yes. I'm fine."

"They weren't right for you, anyway," she said.

He smiled tiredly. She seemed like an old friend, the impassivity of her expression familiar, welcome; but she had left him, he sensed it, had gone farther away than she had ever gone before.

"He used to wear horn-rims," she explained to Calloway. "They made him look dignified."

Calloway laughed.

"Let's get out of here," he said.

It was then they heard the sobs of the surviving boy, whom they had overlooked as they talked. He was sitting on a rock with his face in his hands as if somehow he were ashamed. The wind was blowing his red hair. Johnson went over, sat next to him, put a hand on his shoulder.

"It's all right," he said quietly. "We know how you feel."

For a while, the boy's shoulders continued to shake, and Johnson felt a tightness in his own throat and a gathering sense of loss. He looked up at the sky, where the clouds sped by under the impetus of the quick wind. It would be near twilight, he guessed, by the time the four of them got down. Then he and Calloway would go and together they would bury the dead.

From 1959 to 1961 I was a student in the Writers Workshop at the University of Iowa. This was a wonderful place to be if you were a writer, but not such a good place to be if you were a climber. There were some good limestone cliffs along the Mississippi River near Moline; and, if you were willing to drive further than that, some wonderful quartzite cliffs at Devil's Lake near Madison, Wisconsin.

I was climbing at Devil's Lake one day in 1960 when I met a man, then in his middle fifties, who walked with a cane and who did even the most difficult climbs without a rope. (Unroped climbing was rare in the U.S. in those days.) This man's name, I have since learned, was Dave Slinger. He was a soft-spoken, gentle man who usually climbed alone but who, if you hung around him long enough, would usually agree to do one together. "I don't use a rope for that," he would say, gazing up some 120-foot, nearly vertical cliff, *"but I'd be glad to take one up for you." And you would nod and think:* Is he going to do that without a rope? *And of course he did.*

I once saw Dave Slinger assist two good, roped, climbers who had gotten into a jam halfway up one of the more difficult routes on the cliffs. Slinger, who did his climbing in farmer's boots, climbed to the place where the two young men were stuck, helped unstick them, then proceeded to finish out the climb—all this without a rope.

Dave Slinger made a great impression on me. The story and characters that follow are fiction; but, like most fiction, they have their wellspring in fact.

Written: Phoenix, Arizona; Spring, 1962
First Published: *Phoenix Point West,* March, 1963
Reprinted: *Short Story International,* September, 1965
 Literary Cavalcade (Scholastic Magazines), March, 1967
 The Personal Response to Literature (Houghton Mifflin Company), 1971
 Outsiders: American Short Stories for Students of ESL (Prentice Hall), 1984
 Recorded for the benefit of blind subscribers by *Choice Magazine Listening* in January, 1967

HAWSMOOT

One day at the base of the cliffs high above the Wisconsin lake came a young German climber who carried no rope and said that no one could follow him unroped on a climb of the Grand Giraffe.

"Climbers who are good climb with ropes," he said. "But climbers who are great climb alone."

The German was eighteen and wore *lederhosen* and an orange climbing parka. While he talked his gray eyes sparkled and his lips parted in a smile over his square white teeth, but the smile was as distant as the lake below him and his eyes were as cold as the autumn sun which hung in the sky above him like a frozen amulet.

"I will be great," he said. "So I climb unroped where other climbers will not follow."

Gathered at the base of the cliff hearing the German speak was a group of young men and women with coiled ropes on their shoulders and belts hung with climbing iron. Most of them wore blue parkas or windbreakers with the insignias of climbing clubs sewn on their sleeves. In back of them was one older man who carried no rope or gear or insignia, and who rested on a walking cane. He looked like a trail walker of the Audubon variety.

When the German had finished speaking the young men and women did not answer him, but the older man did.

"I'll follow you," he said.

The young German's eyes softened. The Prussian lines of his jaw relaxed and a shock of blonde hair fell over his forehead.

"Do you climb?" he asked.

The man, who was fifty-four, stepped out from the group of younger people. He was an ordinary looking man with gentle and undistinguished features like those of a regular army

corporal, or a custodian at a school for small children. He wore
an army surplus shirt and pants and soft leather climbing
shoes, and he used the cane when he walked because the pain
in his back was terrible without it.

"I'll follow you," he said.

The German was watching him carefully. "You climb?" he
repeated.

"Sure," the man said.

The German gestured at the cliff behind him. The sleeves
of his parka were rolled back to the elbow and the muscles
of his forearms bulged under the skin like rocks in a silk sock.

"The Giraffe?" he said.

"Sure," the man said.

The German kept smiling as he looked at the man, but his
eyes were like gimlets. The man looked back calmly, wishing
the German would begin to climb, for his back hurt and really he had climbed enough for one day. It was time to drive back
to North Fork and make a meal of corn muffins and franks
and then get under the heat lamp. But the German was arro-
gant and the young climbers, who were quite good, would not
answer the challenge to climb alone because they were used
to the safety of a rope. As for himself, he had climbed on these
cliffs for thirty years; he had done the most difficult climbs,
and never in all that time had he used a rope.

"If you climb the Giraffe," the German said smiling, "even
as far as the overhang, even with a rope for safety, I'll buy you
a supper tonight."

"Sure," the man said. The youth was insulting and cocksure and for a moment the man became angry, until his own
pain and weariness came over him. Then all he wanted to do
was sit down.

"*Ja*," said the German. "Good. It's a good joke."

He walked to the start of the climb and looked up. The
cliff rose nearly vertical a hundred and twenty feet and was
split by a long crack that looked like a lightning bolt. Aside

from the crack the gray rock was quite smooth, broken now and then by small nubbins and ledges where it was possible to place usually no more than one half inch of the sole of a boot. The crack itself was big enough in some places to take a man's hand and in others his fist or toe. Twenty feet from the top a small overhanging roof jutted out from the cliff about four feet. To the people who had first made the climb the long crack resembled the neck of a giraffe and the overhang resembled its head.

"*Ja,*" said the German. "*Es is alles nur Spass.*"

He studied the beginning of the climb, then raised his hands above his head fitting them carefully into the crack. In that attitude he paused for a moment, looking like a brightly colored still from a ballet. "A good one," he said glancing over his shoulder. Then he raised his right foot lightly to a small hold and began to climb.

The man found a rock and sat down resting his chin on his hands which he folded over his cane. *You're right,* he thought as he watched the German climb. *A man can get to be known by climbing without a rope. But maybe I'm too old to climb that way anymore. I don't know. Maybe I am.*

The decision was one he would have to make soon. He knew that. Perhaps he should have made it before now.

The wind blew up from the lake in gusts, up the cliff where it ballooned the orange parka until the German looked huge and then the wind suddenly died and the air went out of the parka and the German looked small again, high on the cliff, sixty feet up, resting on small holds.

"He'll eat crow," one of the young climbers said.

The German yodeled, tilting his head up, a sharp Bavarian yodel that echoed down the cliffs.

"He's an egotistical so-and-so isn't he, Mr. Hawsmoot?" a young girl said.

Bill Hawsmoot smiled. They were nice people these young climbers, and certainly meant well. But there were some things they didn't understand. There were some things that a man decided for himself; about the rope for instance. They had wanted him to use a rope when he climbed. They offered to climb with him every weekend so he would always be sure to have a partner, and when he kept refusing, or tried polite-ly to change the subject, they had thought he was too poor to buy a rope and offered to buy one for him.

The German had begun to climb again moving slowly, high enough up now that a fall would kill him, moving slow-ly but easily the way a squirrel can climb the trunk of a big barked tree. *You are good,* Hawsmoot thought, watching the young German climb. *And they won't offer you a rope because you're young. And I'm old. I guess that's the real difference between you and me.*

The young climbers came to the lake every spring as soon as the ice was off the cliffs. They climbed for a week or two weeks. Some of them climbed all summer until the leaves turned yellow and the air got so cold their hands turned numb on the rock. Not just young climbers either, but young and middle-aged and old. Some came back for a second season. Some came back year after year for four or five years. Then they would disappear and he would never see or hear of them again. In thirty years he had seen so many climbers come and go from the lake that all their faces seemed the same to him, and while he remembered certain climbs he had taught them to do — or had done while they watched gazing up at him like a half circle of interested possums — he could not remember anything particular about them except that most of them climbed well and that all of them used ropes; that each year there would be a few new ones among them, and a few of the old ones would have gone.

He would remember the German. Not the orange parka, or the blonde hair that the wind was whipping up there, or the powerful arms and legs that lifted his weight like jacks, but the fact that the German was making a difficult climb without the protection of a rope. He was already to the overhang, standing on small holds a hundred feet above the ground, so close under the overhang that his head was bent sideways, his cheek pressed flat against the cold stone of the roof.

"He'll see what it's all about now," one of the young climbers said. "The cheese will get more binding."

Some of the others laughed dryly but the sounds were meaningless to Hawsmoot who at this moment was bound body and soul to the climber who clung to the rock so high up that when he dislodged a small pebble it took a long time to hit the ground, and when it did it broke. The orange parka luffed in the breeze which blew up suddenly and then stopped. The dry-leaf rustle on the slope died. A silence came over the cliff. The German moved his left hand out to the edge of the overhang in such silence that Hawsmoot heard his ring scrape against the rock. The right hand followed the left out to the edge. Then he let his feet come away from the wall and swung by his hands four feet out from the cliff like a man on a high trapeze. The group at the base of the cliff watched. The German raised himself up slowly as if to gain the overhang, then lowered himself to arm's length again. The people watching caught their breath. Hawsmoot felt his heart begin to hammer. He had hung like that many times and knew exactly how it felt, like hanging onto life by the fingertips. The German raised himself, paused, then lowered himself again.

"Look at him show off," one of the young men said. "Crazy egotist!"

The German hung motionless above them for a moment longer, then raised himself up again, but not stopping this time, following through by kicking a foot high up, moving with great precision, levering himself up quickly until he stood on top of the roof. Then he finished the last twenty feet and sat at the cliff edge smiling down at them.

When Hawsmoot got up and walked to the start of the climb, one of the girl climbers followed him. There were club insignias sewn to the sleeves of her parka.

"Don't climb without a rope, Mr. Hawsmoot," she said. "You shouldn't."

She was a pretty girl, long dark braids like panther tails almost reached her waist. There were usually a few like her each summer, prettier than most. He tried to remember the one last summer, the one he'd taught to climb the overhang on the Leaning Tower. But he couldn't remember. Maybe it had been the summer before, or any one of thirty summers.

"I guess I'll be all right," he said laying his cane carefully against the cliff as a man who would come back for it. "It's a good climb. I know it pretty well."

The massive cliff was in shadow now for it faced east and the sun had passed behind it. Know it well? Yes, he knew it well. He knew how it looked in all seasons; how it was in sun and shade, in snow and ice. He knew where it was easy to climb and where it was hard, and where, so far at least, it had been impossible. He knew intimately the long crack that looked like the neck of a giraffe, knew the size of each nubbin of rock on either side, how long he could stand on it comfortably, which way it sloped and which foot must be placed on it to make the climb smoothly.

It did not seem surprising to him that he knew the rock so well. The cliffs from end to end measured less than a mile, and he had spent half a lifetime studying them.

The wind blew up in gusts and died and blew again. His back began to throb, the torn muscles drawing up in spasm against the cold. For a minute it seemed to him he had been standing in front of the cliff since spring and that whole seasons had gone by until suddenly it was winter. Foolish, because it had only been a minute or so. He reached his hands over his head and placed them in the crack, a little lower down than the German had, and as soon as a little of his weight was on his hands, his back stopped hurting.

"You shouldn't do it," the girl said. He was startled by her voice so close to him. "We can run up the trail to the top and lower a rope. It wouldn't take long."

"Don't worry about me," he said. "I want to do the climb."

He started. The rock felt good, a little cold which he liked because his hands stuck hard to the holds and did not perspire as they did sometimes in summer. The young climbers were talking below him. He heard them say that Hawsmoot was still one of the best climbers in the country and that the German would eat crow, but soon the words and the sounds of their voices became meaningless and he was alone with his climb as he had been for so many years.

He tried to think just when it was he had begun. It was after the old man had been killed in the brutal accident with the mower. It was after the farm went under, which he remembered so vividly as the day when the auctioneer came out and sold all the furniture and took down the big sign on the barn that said *Hawsmoot.* It was either just before or just after his mother's death, right about the time he took the job in the cannery. He still worked at the cannery, worked on a belt culling the cans that got fouled up in the labeling machine and came out with tattered labels or no labels at all. It was not what he had wanted to do with his life, not at all. But the farm had failed and no better job was open to him. There was no money, and he had to eat.

He reached down to brush some grit from a foothold and watched the pieces fall like drops of water far below him to the ground where the young climbers gazed up at him. From the corner of his eye the forested slope of yellow-leafed trees fell steeply away to the mud shore of the lake. That was right. He remembered now. It was early spring of the year his mother had died when he had come out to the lake to swim and had seen the climbers working the cliffs. He had put on his boots and levis and climbed the steep slope to the cliffs and watched all that afternoon, and he had come back the next day to watch again. This was the sport, better than football or baseball which he had never cared much for. He watched long enough to see how the climbers moved on the rock, then he went off to a cloistered section of the cliffs and began practicing on his own. He had always been shy. Too shy to ask if he could climb with the others.

For the next three years the careful study of the rock, the discovery of force and counterforce and the delicacy of balance, all the myriad techniques of moving up and down steep rock, let him forget the loss of his family and home, and made it easier to work on the belt where he performed his job as a faceless, nameless man, lost like a pebble in the rock pile of the cannery. . . .

The wind blew so hard for a moment that his eyes watered. The overhang was not far above him now. The climb was going nicely and he felt good except that his hands ached a little, probably from the cold. He paused to rest, taking one hand from the rock and putting it in his pocket, letting the stiff tips of his fingers rest in the warm crease of his groin. . . .

Five years had gone by. Sometime, he couldn't remember exactly when or how it happened, he had begun climbing on the big cliffs and gradually the other climbers began to recognize him and they gathered to watch as he climbed the most difficult climbs alone and unroped. Sure. It was a little after that that a short blond-haired man with a stiff brown beard asked to climb with him.

"I'm Joe Meyers," he said. "You're Hawsmoot, aren't you?"

Hawsmoot said yes that was his name, and wondered how this stranger knew it.

"You know all the best climbs, I guess," Meyers said.

"Sure."

"I'd like to climb some of them with you."

"Sure," Hawsmoot said.

They climbed. Without a rope Hawsmoot led climb after climb and Meyers followed. No matter how severe the pitch, Meyers followed with such grace that Hawsmoot knew this man was the best that had ever come to the lake.

At the end of the day when they stood at the base of the highest climb, Hawsmoot pointed up the rock and said, "The overhang is hard."

Meyers nodded. He stood on the ground watching Hawsmoot climb up the crack that looked like a lightning bolt, and when he saw Hawsmoot swing out from the cliff hanging by his hands from the edge of the overhang, feet swinging free, Meyers smiled and shook his head slowly and said, "I'd want a rope for that one." And he did not follow.

It was as clear in Hawsmoot's mind as if it had happened yesterday, or today, as though it were happening again. Joe Meyers. The other climbers told Hawsmoot who he was. He was one of the five best climbers in the country, and he had hitchhiked from California to see Hawsmoot climb.

"How'd he know my name?" Hawsmoot had asked.

A girl had replied a little disdainfully, "Everybody knows you."

Others came. Peters from Utah, Turner from Colorado, Mrs. Ann Brisket from Anchorage, Dietrich from Austria, Steffano from Italy; famous climbers on their way to make first ascents in all the mountain ranges of the hemisphere stopped at the lake to see Hawsmoot climb, the man they had heard of who did extreme climbs unroped.

Himself, he had never been thirty miles beyond his own town. But these climbers brought the world to him and took him to the world. . . .

He was about to smile thinking this when suddenly he saw something above him, blocking his way. He was startled and for the first time he grew tense on his holds. What the hell.

It was the overhang, that's all it was. But it seemed to loom over his head, dark and fatal looking. Until now he had hardly been conscious of the climb, his hands and feet working automatically. Now he must keep his mind on the rock. He inched up until his head was bent under the overhang and his cheek rested against the cold stone roof. No need to hurry here, there's time. Far down there he could see the young climbers gazing up like possums, and behind them the slope of trees dropped into the lake. It gave him the impression of being a thousand feet up, so high up in the heavens he wanted to let go, fall back into the soft oblivion of a cloud. He was very still, hugging the stone closely, his cheek pressed against it as if he were embracing a close friend he was leaving and knew he might not see again.

Then the left hand moved out to the edge of the roof and caught in the familiar hold, the rock gritty against his nails. Then the right hand went slowly out to meet the left; and instantly after that his feet pulled from the wall.

Hawsmoot! Hawsmoot! Something was wrong. He kept hearing his name, someone was shouting his name, and his arms weren't working. The wind was blowing from the lake so cold it numbed his hands and his arms weren't pulling him up. He dangled above the ground, confused, alarmed. He felt a great desire to drop off, to let go; and he was weary, tired out. It had just been too much for one day, too damn much. He was exhausted. But he forced the arms to work until slowly by inches his head was level with his hands. He forced the arms again, forced them so hard he thought the muscles would burst through the skin, forced them until his waist was level with his hands. Wobbling, he kicked his shoe up, and missed the hold. He hung out over the emptiness, hung out over the abyss with every fiber of his body screaming to let go. But he kicked again and this time made it. He pressed his weight up on that leg and reached for higher hand holds. He was over.

On top of the overhang, he rested. It had not been close, only a little clumsy missing the foothold the first time. Plenty of good young climbers had missed that hold and fallen from the overhang, caught by their ropes. *You should climb with a rope, Mr. Hawsmoot.* He had climbed it many times, a hundred times, at least that. He had first climbed it when he was thirty and the only difference now was that he climbed it more slowly and had missed the foothold the first time. Had they been calling his name? He guessed not. They were standing down there, so far now that they were hard to make out, dim white faces all the same. *Mr. Hawsmoot, use a rope.*

It was getting to be twilight and he felt saddened at the thought of having to walk the hiking trail back to the base of the cliff without a cane, his back sore in the damp evening air. He did not think about making the German eat crow, the German was all right. He was young and cocksure and good, and probably he had little money and was trying to make a name for himself in the States. The German was all right. What he thought about as he stood on the steep cliff high above the ground was that this year he would be fifty-five, and sixty in five years; and that one day his hands would not hold. *You should wear a rope, Mr. Hawsmoot.* Yes, that would save him all right.

He looked at his hands on the knobby rock and thought of the lifetime he had spent building their power. He thought of Meyers coming from California to climb with him. He thought of Dietrich, Steffano, Peters, and all the others who had come to see him climb. He thought of the faceless, nameless hundreds who had come to the lake to climb roped and had left forgotten. *You should wear a rope. Maybe so. Maybe I'm too old to climb without one. Maybe it was close just now, I don't know.* He began climbing again, the last twenty feet.

The German was waiting at the top of the cliff. When he came forward his face seemed softer in the shadows. They stood facing each other in the stiff wind that blew up the cliffs causing the leaves to make sounds like pebbles down tin chutes.

"You are a great climber," the German said. "If I had known . . . ."

"I guess we better get down the trail before dark," the man said. He did not want the German to feel humble.

"Yes," the German said. "Surely. My name is Fuchs, and yours . . . ."

"Hawsmoot."

The sound of that name as it fell from his lips carried from the cliffs out over the land to the shores of seas and beyond. It beaconed his soul. It carried his decision. Go on climbing without the rope. Go on climbing as always. Hope I am high up when the hands don't hold.

When I left the Writers Workshop at the University of Iowa, Nancy and I moved to Phoenix, Arizona. I taught English and Writing at Phoenix College for a while, then became editor of the city magazine.

Very early in the spring of 1961, I climbed Mt. Humphries, the highest of the San Francisco Peaks (12,700') near Flagstaff, Arizona. The climb was basically a long and pleasant hike uphill. The upper mountain was snow-covered and deserted, the only tracks visible my own. The approach to the summit was up a graceful, curving, snow-covered ridge. I was very much taken by the beauty of this ridge and knew, even while I was climbing it, that I would want to try and write a story in which it could become a part.

In the early years of my career, as soon as I would finish writing a short story, I would put it in an envelope and airmail it to the New Yorker. *I would then wait in a sort of feverish impatience for the* New Yorker *to respond. They always responded promptly and always in the same way: with a very small, very polite form rejection slip. I would then send my story to most of the other national magazines; and once it had been rejected by all of them, I would start working my way through the quarterlies.*

At one point, several years after I had written "The Rhyme of Lancelot," it was accepted by an obscure quarterly based in Chicago. Many months passed with no word from the editor. At the end of half a year, I sent him a post card, asking if everything was all right. He sent the story back by return mail, saying he had never had any use for impatient writers. Six years passed before I finally placed "The Rhyme of Lancelot" in the South Dakota Review.

Two years later the story was selected to be reprinted in Best Little Magazine Fiction: 1970.

Written: Phoenix, Arizona; Winter, 1962
First Published: *South Dakota Review,* Autumn, 1968
Reprinted: *Best Little Magazine Fiction: 1970* (New York
    University Press)

THE RHYME OF LANCELOT

He was sixty. She was fifty-five. Four years ago she had come into the bank to make a will, and he had helped her with it and during the course of things in a most natural way he had asked her to have tea with him at the coffee shop across from the bank, and she had accepted. They had understood each other at once for they were both unhappy, and gradually they grew affectionate, and finally they grew intimate. The affair began in the fourth year of their friendship, and they carried it on through the three months of autumn. Like the season, it was getting old.

"What are you doing, Jame?" he asked. He sat in his shorts and sleeveless undershirt, and looked through the clean squares of the motel window to the place where the mountain began.

"Setting my hair," she said from the bath. "You're a caveman you know; it's a mess."

"We should go on our walk," he said. "Before we leave, I mean."

She came into the room where he sat, opening a bobby pin with her teeth. Her hair was soft gray. She wore a half slip and stockings, but her wrinkled breasts were bare and he looked at them thoughtfully.

"We don't have to walk," she said. "I always liked it though. It was part of us."

"Well of course we'll walk." He was agitated at her use of past tense so he fiddled with a Gideon Bible that lay on the writing desk. "Jame," he said.

"Yes."

"It's not like it was at first. I mean it's not as good as when we began."

She sat down at the edge of the bed, covering herself with her arms.

"I guess it isn't, Michael. But I thought it was still fun."

He opened and closed the Gideon Bible and he said, " Fun. You know, I think that's exactly the right word. Three months ago it was exciting for an old couple, and in so short a time it's gone to fun." He shook his head. "A few more months and it could be indifference. It could be our marriages all over again."

She had taken her lip in her teeth and he saw that she was upset. "It's not your fault, Jame," he said. He got up and put his arm around her. "It's not our fault; it's just the way things are, I guess."

"We've always understood each other," she said. "Perhaps we're just having a bad day."

He nodded. At times like this, she seemed like a stranger. Something was wrong. Either they had lost something, or they hadn't progressed. At this point in his life he was sensitive to the failures in a relationship.

"There's nothing at home for either of us," he said almost to himself. "The very best, the nicest we have is what we have here."

"I know it is."

"Jame," he said eagerly, turning to look at her again. "Do you know what it was like the first time between us? I felt like a god!"

She laughed and her eyes sparkled at him. "You're always dramatic," she said.

"I don't care, damn it, I mean it." He went to the window and looked out again at the high slopes. "And now; well it's like getting to the top of something and having to come down. Let's fight it, Jame." He went back to her. "Let's not have a bad thing happen again."

"What will we do?"

"All right. Instead of taking our usual walk, which we've taken eighteen times, by the way, we'll do something different.

Let's climb the mountain." He was pleased with himself; it was like throwing down the glove.

"Why we can't do that," she said. "There isn't time. It will be dark soon."

"We'll go tomorrow, first thing."

She laughed. "Michael, you crazy man. You know I have to be back tonight."

"Call. Make an excuse."

"I can't," she said. "Really."

He took her shoulders in his hands and stared at her.

"But Jame, what did you do the first time when we decided to come here?"

"I made an excuse," she said. "I guess I could make another."

That afternoon, for the nineteenth time, they took their walk arm in arm through the village; but now there were differences. Instead of looking in at the shoe shop and commenting on prices and styles, they went in and rented two pairs of boots and bought wool socks. At the market, where they usually stopped to sniff the fresh vegetable smells, they went in and spent almost an hour picking fruits and cheeses for an alpine lunch. They bought a pint bottle of claret and a small box of cashews. On the way back to the room, they made a brief stop at the pay telephone, and in the motel office arrangements were made to spend an extra night. For supper, instead of going to the usual restaurant, they drove into the next town and found a German beer cellar that served knockwurst and dark beer. Their time together in the room that night did not regain its lost dimensions, but it showed promise, and he fell asleep in the early hours satisfied that the direction of the affair had changed.

They awoke early, pleased to get up and be doing something. He tucked his trousers into the wool socks so they looked like climbing knickers, and he wore a green flannel shirt and his reindeer sweater. She put on a blue wool skirt and blouse, and drew her socks up to her knees.

"Jame," he said. "You can't climb a mountain in your skirt."

"Well why not?"

"It just isn't done. We should have bought you a pair of slacks."

She laughed. "Well it's not a very big mountain is it? They say there's a trail to the top. Besides, it will be something new."

"That's right," he said. "And if things get rough I can give you mine, and go on in my shorts." He put his arms around her and held her close. "Things could have been different; if only we had met with our lives in front of us."

She put her hand over his mouth. "We promised not to go on about things that aren't possible."

"I know, damn it. There's no point."

They put on their coats and tramped through the village to have breakfast at the all night diner. She ordered a poached egg on toast, and he had a stack of pancakes, which he always considered a man's breakfast although they did not agree with him.

"We've put new life into us, Jame," he whispered to her over their empty plates. "It's good again."

"It's not like pumping up a tire," she said, but he saw that she was happy.

From the diner, they went across town to the city park where the trail to the mountain began. The sky was bright and western with a fine sun beginning to rise. He wiggled his fingers in his driving gloves and his toes in the good-fitting boots.

"Not cold?" he asked.

"No, I feel wonderful. It was a good idea of yours, Michael."

"Have you ever climbed a mountain before?" he asked.

She thought for a moment. "Never one this big," she said.

He smiled. "Neither have I. I'm glad it's you and me."

She touched his arm.

The trail was easy to follow, a slender line of dirt twisting upwards through the heavy forest of pines that covered the lower slopes. At first they walked briskly, but soon they slowed their pace and he reminded her that they were not young. She walked along in front of him, her hands in her coat pockets. He followed, watching the trees and stones for a while, but soon losing himself in his thoughts. He thought about many things, and when he thought about something particularly vital, he gestured with his hands as though his mind were an orchestra and he were conducting. He loved Jame. It was a simple orderly fact, the kind he liked, uncluttered and clean. He wanted to know what Jame thought about him. He knew she liked him very well, but he wanted to know exactly.

"Michael," she said. "Have you noticed the jays?"

"Yes, they're lovely," he said. "Proud looking devils."

"I saw a cardinal a while back, but you were woolgathering."

"Damn it," he said. "I've always liked cardinals. Be sure I'm in on the next one."

They climbed on in silence. On the steep sections the trail switchbacked, making it easier to gain elevation. The trees began to thin and the ground was strewn with rocks and boulders. He thought they were going very slowly, but soon they began to see patches of snow, and at one rest stop they had a view of the summit, white against a dark blue sky.

Michael walked and waved his hands. It was hard for Jame. She had not been raised to carry on with a man, and he thought the lines in her face had grown deeper and longer in the last three months. But it had been Jame who suggested the first weekend, and he had been shocked and delighted for he never thought they could be more than friends. And they were still just friends. She always reminded him of that. Love was elusive and full of sadness. He remembered the story of Paolo and Francesca when Dante asked them why they were in hell and Francesca said they had read the Rhyme of Lancelot and sinned. And Paolo had wept.

"Jame," Michael said, puffing badly. The last stretch had

winded him and he guessed the air was getting thin. "Let's have lunch." They had been climbing three hours.

"Should I pick a spot?" she asked.

"Why don't you," he said.

They went a little way off the trail to a clearing where the sun beamed brightly on a carpet of pine needles and cones. She took a kerchief from the pocket of her coat and spread it on the ground. He brought out the fruits and cheeses and pared equal servings with a one-bladed silver pocket knife that the bank had given him in memory of something he had done; he could not remember what. Two chipmunks gathered to chitter for scraps while they ate their snack in the rich odors of pine sap and earth.

Sitting in the sun warmed Michael, and he was able to take off his driving gloves; and then all at once, as he began to peel an orange, it occurred to him that he and Jamie seldom talked to each other. They took their pleasures in mere presence, and he supposed that was the finest thing two people could do who were approaching the eventide of disappointed lives.

He breathed in deeply the resin smell of outdoors and took a tangy wedge of cheese between his teeth. It was a damn nice picnic they were having. A very pleasant, happy time.

He had been born on the eastern coast, not far from Plymouth Rock. He had been raised in the New England traditions; he had married, and sired a son. He had spent thirty years working in a bank. He had been to the funerals of four generations of his family, and during his lifetime he had read of two wars and a police action. For sixty years he had known consciousness; he could measure the time easily, seven hundred and twenty months, three thousand one hundred and twenty weeks, twenty-one thousand nine hundred days. A long time. Yet, when he ranged the still clear beam of his memory through the long wilderness of lost years, he could say quite truthfully that eating a wedge of cheese on the slope of a mountain with his lady friend in the twilight of his time was one of a small total of moments that he could say had been happy.

"You know, Jame," he said. "I think a god watches over you and me."

"We're just old sinners," she said. "We'll be roasted on a spit one day." She looked very peaceful, he thought; the sun had brought an attractive flush to her cheeks.

"Why damn it," he said. "The old man, if he is up there, what could he find wrong with a picnic."

"The picnic's all right," she said. She looked momentarily worried, and he knew what she was thinking.

"You don't suppose the old peep can see through the motel roof, do you?" He grinned at her.

"Michael," she said quite sternly. "Don't court trouble with the Lord."

When they passed timberline, they could look down to the valley and see the buildings of the village nestled there, a few columns of smoke hazing up from chimneys. They walked very slowly now because the air was thin, and they were tired. Once, he saw a gum wrapper on the side of the trail and when he stooped to pick it up he felt a pain in his back and hoped that his disc wouldn't go out. They saw black ravens spiraling on air cushions up into the sheer sky, and chipmunks go tense on lichen-covered rocks as they passed. Then all at once and not knowing it would happen, they saw the arc of the summit ridge spread out before them like a scimitar moon.

"Michael," she said. "Isn't that the top? Over there I mean."

"Yes. We're almost there."

The ridge was covered with snow, and he led the way, letting his feet make their marks in the clean white powder. She followed in his train. In half an hour they had reached the top and could look back along the long path they had made in the snow that arced away from them.

She looked at it a moment, and then she said, "I think it's the most beautiful thing I have seen."

He had wanted to make love to her right there on the summit, but he knew it was too cold and they were too tired so he got out the claret and cashews and they had a snack.

Then he took her in his arms and kissed her a long kiss until his heart beat fiercely in the thin summit air, and when their lips came apart in a cloud of frosty breath she said, "I love you, Michael."

She had never said this to him before, and when he heard the words he knew how much he had needed and wanted to hear them. And it was right between them again. Whatever it was they had begun to lose yesterday in the valley, they had regained today on the mountain top.

For a long while he held her in his arms and gazed through the blowing strands of her hair to a world of mountains that ranged the corridors of his vision. Then, because there was nothing else to do, and because it was getting late, he took her by the hand and led her down familiar tracks.